I0567031

American Evolution

Adolescence of a Nation

By Sheri Dixon

Copyright 2013 by the author- no part of this book may be reproduced without the author's permission

"Courage is found in unlikely places."
— J.R.R. Tolkien

"It is not the strongest of the species that survives,
nor the most intelligent, but rather the one most
adaptable to change."
—Dr. Leon C. Megginson

"Well I won't back down
No I won't back down
You can stand me up at the gates of hell
But I won't back down"
— Tom Petty

Sheri Dixon

Foreward

We live in interesting and scary times. From our environment to our economy to our health everything is spinning out of our hands and out of our control.

Stubbornly we cling to what we're familiar with, even if it's not good for us…even if it's killing us. Because what we see now we assume to be the way things have always been.

In an effort to feel less powerless in the face of great changes, it's natural to fantasize about grandiose "what ifs" and we're inundated by superhuman tales of ordinary men (it's almost exclusively men) who rise to the occasion and literally save the world when the world is teetering over the edge of sanity.

But this cultural shift is nothing new. From the moment humans appeared societies have risen and fallen, expanded and imploded. It's happened before and will happen again.

Society changes in tiny ways and in huge leaps every day, and all of that is more normal than not. Think of the huge changes we've seen in the last hundred years. The last Fifty. The last ten. Anything is possible. Most things are probable.

The reality is that under stress people are just as likely to behave well as to behave badly.

Yet we assume the worst as the fictitious guns blazing vigilante rides in to save the day either alone or with big-hearted big-muscled back up, all wielding an arsenal to literally die for as their pretend society plunges (oddly immediately) into total chaos.

What about the small ones? The quiet and unassuming souls who have no power to begin with? Where are their life experiences recorded? Are they less important, less memorable?

When my grandmother was 8 her house didn't have electricity, a telephone or running water. When my mother was 8 she rode the milk route with the milkman because she loved the horse that pulled his wagon. I remember getting our first color TV when I was about 8, and when my daughter was 8 no one had home computers or video games.

Follow four young girls- four generations of a family, through the next few possible phases of mankind.

On Thanksgiving Day.

Backwards.

The heroes make the story books.

The rest of us make history.

Sheri Dixon

<u>Prologue</u>

"And they lived happily ever after".

The well-worn book closed gently of its own accord, and all was quiet. The words shimmered for an instant in everyone's minds and then dissipated-leaving a residue of peace and contentment behind.

Crispin smiled at her family gathered around her for Thanksgiving and it was good.

Breathing in the clear clean spring air, the aroma of honeysuckle gave it weight and heft so it seemed as though the air breathed through her lungs, not the other way around. Every breath she took caught in her lungs just a bit- it had been that way for seemingly ever but lately had gotten just a little worse every day, and every motion of her old body seemed to creak and groan, although she knew it only echoed in her own ears.

She'd seen many Thanksgivings- well over 80, but was determined to see a few more yet. Her life had finally and for certain gotten to the good part and she refused to let go of it…at least for a while.

She sat at the head of the table, the place of honor- the place of the Matriarch.

Her hair was pulled back and up, but still managed to escape in unruly tendrils that glinted honey gold and brushed silver in the sunlight. Her dress was flowing and loose to cover most of the effects of natural gravity over the years as well as the souvenirs of years past- scars worn to silver but still visible, places her bones had not healed quite right. The soft plain cotton had been embroidered with vines of the palest green, tiny leaves and blossoms seemed to glow with a life of their own, encircling her gently and beautifully.

Around her neck she wore a pendant of green amber twined in tiny twigs of silver- signifying her bond with the Earth. Her ring was Moldavite- a faceted meteor harnessed into an endless knot, and her sterling bracelet bore the symbols of her family and home. Sparkling in her ear lobes were small green Amethysts- the stone of spirituality and serenity. Together these pieces were more than adornment; they had all been her mother's and they were talismans that gave her direction and protection.

Her feet were bare, as was the custom.

 The sun still felt strange on her face- warm and welcoming. For so many years any natural light at all had been cold as steel and just as nurturing, leaking sickly through the smog, reluctantly. It was lovely to bask luxuriantly, absorbing the healing warmth that eased the aches in her bones, the pains in her muscles.

With the shift in the atmosphere, the sky was more violet than blue and the leaves of plants were just a tad more orange than green. Blossoms were smaller but more fragrant and seeds and nuts were more compact, but also more nutrient-dense.

Evolution.

People and animals, too, were just a little different. Physically each generation was a bit smaller in stature from a diet that contained more vegetative matter than protein, but their health did not suffer because there was no such thing as an empty calorie.

Food was not scarce, but never wasted. Water was plentiful, but precious. Nothing was taken for granted.

Though at 83 years old Crispin's eyes were weaker now, her hearing not so good, her step less sure, her heart remained strong and filled with wonder at her life; their life. Her family. They lived as all others did now, in multi-generational family communities. Shelters close enough to each other for convenience but far enough apart for privacy, each little band somehow managed to achieve the balance of talent and skills necessary to not only survive, but thrive.

It was this physical closeness of blood relatives without the constant bombardment of distractions from the outer world that uncovered and accentuated the ability they all seemed to have to mentally connect with others in their group. All of the family communities had it, this connection with their own others. Not mind-reading or anything invasive or threatening, this was more of a gentle touch, a reassurance of knowing where loved ones were and being able to tell them everything was fine. That they were never alone.

Placing the book tenderly in front of her, her hands lingered for a moment on the surface of the table, and she could feel the vibrations from the energy still trapped in the giant log. This too, was something everyone could do, that everyone did do almost without thinking now. For almost a dozen generations humans had lost the ability to bond with each other and their world and it had gone badly for them.

Luckily that was but a drop in the bucket of their existence and was easily recalled and relearned.

Luckily they had ever so narrowly evaded tipping over into "too late".

The enormous tree had been felled by a particularly violent storm- lightening splitting the massive trunk completely in two- half tipped into the river and was swept away and the other half crashed onto the ground right here. They'd planed it and sanded it, oiled it and burnished it and it served them royally for meals both casual and formal.

She lifted her eyes and her thoughts to the celebration at hand, and she visually brushed across each beloved face down the long side of this fallen forest giant.

Her daughter Eliza's attention was on the food in the center of the table- traditional foods of the Springtime Thanksgiving. Covering one platter, tender new shoots and greens radiated around diced, seasoned and simmered root crops from the previous fall in a show of gratitude for enough food through the winter before the new growth of spring. Steamed fish and roasted chicken were surrounded by boiled eggs and crayfish on another. Tender flat breads waited to be filled with each person's preferred combination of the bounty.

Herbal tea steeped in a large earthen tea pot that had been stained violet and orange with shiny blue flecks- a pottery sunset. Smaller matching drinking bowls orbited it, waiting their turn.

Carved wooden dishes of fresh berries were arranged off to the side for an after dinner treat, next to smaller flat breads that had been sweetened with honey. Her critical eyes softened and the smile lines showed around them when she was satisfied that everything was there, in the right place, and in abundance.

It had not always been so in her lifetime. The time of the Liberation had seen much hunger and loss, and the fear of those times was instilled into Eliza's personality no matter how many years had passed.

Eliza's husband Griffin concentrated on the grandchildren in his lap. Little Fern and her brother Hawk sat in stunned silence as their grandfather pulled first pebbles, then acorn caps from behind their own ears. They exploded in gales of laughter when he balanced a pebble topped with an acorn top hat on his own nose and they soon followed suit, the performance causing Eliza to glare at the three with mock seriousness- her smile clearly breaking through her stern countenance. Griffin was a parlor magician of the highest order when entertainment was needed, but it was Griffin who was consulted about when to plant the crops, to build, to make journeys. He could read the stars and the moon, sense changes in the weather and foretell upcoming storms.

Next to the empty chairs the children should've been occupying, their parents- Eliza's daughter Hope and her husband Darius were oblivious to the rest- even after 2 children and almost 10 years of marriage they held hands and whispered together. Growing up during the Destruction as they had, people of their generation seemed to live just a little more intensely, a bit more deliberately conscious of their mates, never taking them for granted. Because you just never knew.

Hope had embroidered Crispin's dress and people came not only from nearby Unity, but beyond- bringing plain cloth to Hope, and knowing that they'd leave with something uniquely perfect for whatever they were going to use it for. She'd ask about its intended wearer and what type of clothing was to be made of it, gathered up the cloth and started quietly humming, her eyes and fingers feeling the fabric. The pattern spoke to her and she wrote with needle and thread, intuition placing each stitch exactly where it needed to be.

As payment she received something in return according to the talents of the customer. It was always perfect and always something they could use and cherish.

Darius kept the livestock. He knew each animal and their quirks and habits. He could tell by watching, listening and touching if they were healthy or not, stressed or relaxed, and he was able to calm them and nurture them effortlessly and without restraints or force. The animals knew they were being treated in a humane manner by someone who truly cared about and respected them, and they supplied the family with food in a mostly symbiotic manner- the goats giving milk and the chickens giving eggs. The advent of a querulous rooster in the flock heralded a chicken dinner for everyone.

As tradition dictated, the opposite side of the long table was set for those attending from a different realm- the spirit folk both of the woods and their own ancestors. The forest breathed a life of its own, and the humans lived so close to it that they were a part of it- could hear and feel it pulsing in their own veins. The spirit of the forest was welcome at their table alongside the memories of those who had slipped away- sometimes quietly and sometimes against their will, no matter how strong their will had been, during those awful times that had come before.

Her gaze froze as it skimmed two of the vacant chairs; for just an instant Crispin saw her daughter Jane- laughing and animated, filled with her passion for life and next to her was Crispin's own mother with her always kind eyes and gentle smile. Crispin blinked in amazement and they were gone, their voices muted and mingling with the others' till they were intertwined and vanished.

Finally, Crispin looked directly across the table, and her eyes met and locked with Gabriel's. His silver hair flowed onto his shoulders freely, and he sat straight and tall- his deep blue shirt both simple and elegant- long sleeved to cover the scars he also bore. His elbows were on the table, hands clasped together, chin resting on his hands nonchalantly- the very picture of nobility. After all these years her heart still jumped just a bit at the sight of him, in happiness and desire, still and always.

Gabriel smiled at Crispin and he tried not to let his own eyes betray his worry.

They were the same age, but she'd been through so much more than he.

Just beneath the surface of her peaceful countenance, under the lovingly embroidered dress and behind the safety of her talismans, the physical and mental demons of The Reclamation showed plainly if you knew what to look for, and Gabriel knew what to look for- he had lived it with her- shifting shadows of darkness that Crispin kept at bay mostly unconsciously now.

It had become second nature.

Second Nature 2090- Fern

The sounds of Life reverberated from tree to tree and back again.

Leaves rustled enticingly, and then chastised the squirrels careening from branch to branch willy nilly, hither and yon. Birds called to and echoed each other- sounding for information.

Quiet murmurs of adults talking interspersed with the occasional peal of children's laughter. Somewhere music was being played and sung to- very casual, very free-form melodies laced together with words flowing random and unstilted, male and female, elder and child, natural as the birdsong, light as the breeze.

The source of the voices and music seemed hidden at first, the people so easy among the trees that they blended right in. Living *in* the forest, it would never occur to them that they owned it or dominated it- the forest was their home and provided all their needs as a Mother, not a servant. Their shelters too, reflected that sentiment of belonging- small and low, walls curved for strength, not a single straight line or sharp corner stood out among the plant life to catch the eye like a splinter.

Built sturdily years before from the rubble that was left, packed in and dragged into the clearing by hand, the broken cement "stones" had been chiseled and dry stacked, then chinked where necessary with the clay earth. Thatched roofs overhung the walls far enough that the clay mortar was safe from the rains and after just a few seasons the native vines overtook them all and trailed up the walls, cascaded over the windows and shimmied up the roofs, disappearing into the trees.

Like the humans, they were virtually invisible.

Windows and doors, wood planking and furniture, vessels and dishes had all made their way from the abandoned 'old style' houses sinking squalidly into the untended lawns of decaying subdivisions for lack of upkeep and became part of the 'new style' shelters-shelters that had been built with an eye on the sun and prevailing winds, with an awareness of the inhale and exhale of the yearly cycle and an acceptance to work with the seasons instead of fighting them- shelters that looked decidedly inadequate according to the old history and sociology books, but these were the living blueprints for a future without artificial dependency on industrial convenience .

There was no road, per se. A foot path led from one shelter to another and then into the forest. The forest path led eventually to a larger community named Unity just a few miles away that provided the things they couldn't grow or make for themselves, and they bartered fairly and without malice. A trip into Unity was a special occasion that meant meeting new people and old friends, the obtainment of things needed as well as a few special items and treats.

Once in town, children ran free from place to place, exploring and socializing. All the adults watched out for them, bigger children took care of younger ones and no one was excluded from anything for lack or excess of years.

Children were respected as members of the community, and reciprocated by acting in a responsible manner- there was no vandalism or shoplifting, so no need for punishment or threats of punishment.

In years past, such a society was considered primitive and naïve. Now it was recognized as being ultimately civilized.

While they still had the means to replicate the old technological ways- the knowledge was there as were all the old bits and parts that used to literally run society, a conscious choice had been made to leave all that behind- the bad had outweighed the good by a long shot and with tragic results.

Morally, sensibly, economically, the way of Second Nature was better and healthier- a culture too immersed in things and machines quickly becomes impatient and callous towards fallible and fragile organic beings.

When the value of something is measured by artificial means, a life becomes worthless in very short order.

Far from cowardly and backwards, the decision to move forward in a different direction took more courage and willpower than sliding back into the old lazy selfish routines.

There were still cars, busses and trains for trips of longer distances, but the rarity and expense of fuel made mass transit and just a few shared vehicles not only appealing, but necessary.

And there were still people who cheated, and lied, and hurt other people but they were an overwhelming minority. A society that no longer values violence and selfishness in business transactions and as a form of hierarchal power, and which no longer worships a jealous and spiteful god will naturally shift away from those things.

If those aggressive traits are no longer admirable or even acceptable, people will be less likely to do them. That's human nature- to bend to peer pressure.

It took a mass conviction of the sort previously dedicated to religion or politics to recognize and then move forward in the exact opposite direction of what they'd been used to.

But religion had done it to control people's minds.

Politics had done it to control people's bodies.

And now they were doing it to reverse the damage done by religion and politics.

Fern was eight years old. She and her brother Hawk
had been born in one of the family shelters with their
grandmother Eliza the Healer in attendance and they
knew nothing of anything else, or that the gracious
and peaceful way they lived had been at one time
referred to as 'savage'.

The adults in their family group spent their days
tending the garden, the orchard, the small holding of
chickens and dairy goats- lacking electricity for
refrigeration anything that couldn't be consumed by
their group was used for bartering in Unity. Fruits
and vegetables were dried and carefully stored for use
over the winter, and having small stock meant that
harvests were small and manageable- between the
several families they could easily consume the milk
of a few goats, eat a few chickens, scramble up a
dozen eggs. Having something as large as a dairy
cow, beef steer or hog would be wasteful as well as
too taxing on their environment- living in the forest
meant no wide open fields for grazing so the
browsing goats and self-sufficient chickens were
more sensible.

In the beginning, there was grave concern that their
food would not be sufficient once winter set in, but
between careful drying and storage of crops, hunting
and fishing, and the small livestock, there was plenty.
Eliza knew the forest and the plant life in it, and part
of every child's education was to follow her around
and learn how to "shop" the forest for food- she
regularly harvested herbs for medicines and knew

what was edible and what was not- living as they did in a truly temperate climate where snow did not cover the ground all winter was something they were all thankful for- especially now that in many places, there was snow cover almost year round, and in others not enough water to sustain gardens.

Fern was sturdy and solid, just like the shelters, and Hawk was slender and slight but as tough as the vines that covered them. They spent their days like the other children- with their parents, grandparents and great-grandparents, learning the daily routines of living and spending time being read to- books were magical and treasured and they both looked forward to the day that they would take their place reading to the younger children and older folks whose eyes refused to focus on words anymore.

Losing the ability to read the books was a loss every older person faced, but like everything else in life it was looked upon as a transition to something else instead of a tragedy. Not being able to read meant more time spent with the younger people, and that was precious, too. Being read to by those you taught to read was one more example of everything going round and round in the never-ending circle of life.

Every home had a book shelf in a place of honor containing books of all types- fiction and non-fiction, history, art, science…

Even very tiny children reverently yet eagerly poured over the diagrams and photographs of the science books and marveled at the colors and patterns in the art books, and what was on the pages fueled discussions, sparked questions, fanned imaginations way before the words were read.

Just grasping a book- any book, transmitted a feeling of power. Not dark or suffocating, but a power of knowledge for its own sake, demanding to be shared. It was this power that had led to the incineration of millions of books during the Liberation, along with many of the librarians who valiantly tried to prevent it.

Hawk and Fern were typical children. They shared. They got along. There was very little squabbling and bickering because those things come from want and need and they knew neither. Born at home, to parents who labored at or near home, they were secure and sheltered and the result of that was a generation of children who were self-assured and outgoing, who were independent and inquisitive. They were surrounded by all they needed and had no desire to want more.

The young adults had grown up without formal education or religion and were now raising their own children the same way; which was normal, life as usual for them as every generation considers what surrounds them as normal, no matter how flawed it is. Every person in these families had worth and valid ideas- even the very young and the very old. Respect of others was a given, not an aberration.

The older adults remembered differently.

The very old remembered the Reclamation, their children remembered the Liberation and their grandchildren remembered the Destruction. Great-grandchildren were the product of the present, the gift of today.

Part of the education of every child was learning every detail of all three periods in history, and without the glossy slanting that went into the old history books pre-Reclamation. The old history books were flag-waving fairy tails filled with the glory and magnanimous nature of the Homeland, while totally ignoring the cost of war, the innocent bystanders, and the co-lateral damages. Those books had all been written by the victors, not the vanquished.

After the Liberation there were no victors left in the land of liberty.

Children of Hawk's and Fern's age were the very first to be born into Second Nature- the next phase of a New America.

The older adults hoped fervently that the lessons learned would not ever be un-learned no matter how many generations were to come. They held out some ray of hope that it was possible- history had shown that even before the Reclamation, actually all throughout human civilization, there have been bands, tribes and societies of people, isolated by geography, that had managed to survive and thrive until their

Sheri Dixon

discovery by explorers, missionaries and armies introduced them to technology and religion.

Technology spawned envy and religion instilled shame.

Envy and shame are not natural- they are taught emotions. People who are not envious or shamed cannot be controlled and that's what Power is all about- control.

Control of the market. Collectively and consciously people in truly democratic situations work together for the common good.

That's a tough sell.

So from time immemorial, people who were too simple to know what they were missing had to be taught, counseled, *saved* from their dismal communal existence. Groups without leaders, communities without segregation, all anathema to snake oil and salvation salesmen.

Once they are enlightened as to how miserable they are, they can be sold and marketed to. Stuff, things, eternal life- divide and conquer in the name of profit.

Although there had been wars and disasters all through human history, other than the Great Flood there had never been a complete renewal for an entire population until now, when by both happenstance and design, the country was totally isolated from the rest of the world. After every other conflict and correction there were always contingents and pockets of the old ways of thinking- the old ways of forcing the will of the few onto the many.

Every so often, before the Reclamation, small groups would gather and go off into the wilderness (or at least a few miles from the rest of society) and form intentional communities. These were good in theory but since the group members still lived at least part of the time in the existing society, the flaws and imperfections, petty jealousies and egos always wormed their way into the fabric of these brave little attempts at being fully human, and they were tattered and frayed from within, dissolving in disillusion.

Just prior to, and during the Reclamation, small groups formed that isolated themselves from the whole yet they remained steadfastly in the grip of their established ideas and pecking orders. They relied on fear and superstition to keep order, and without exception the intolerant and suspicious nature of their residents caused them to turn on themselves.

The lucky ones made it out alive- physically anyway.

Second Nature was a completely fresh slate, and although it appeared to be soft and passive, the courage and will to deny and decry violence as an answer to anything was its backbone and strength.

It remained to be seen if it could endure beyond the lives of those who remembered anything else.

Fern was the stereotypical big sister- keeping an eye out for her smaller brother, but not to be sure that no one picked on him, because that was unheard of nowadays. With no centralized and segregated schooling, there were no age-specific peer groups. Children of all ages played together and learned together; bigger children looking after and helping smaller ones.

So Fern didn't have to guard her brother from others, she had to make sure that he didn't self-destruct all on his own.

Tiny, wiry, and quick as a thought, Hawk climbed and ran and got into more possible trouble than anyone had ever seen before from a twenty year old, much less a five year old.

As soon as breakfast was finished, Fern blinked and Hawk was gone. Sighing heavily, she wondered how on earth someone who was so small seemed to fly from place to place and she took her dishes and his to the washing sink, gave them a good rinse and scrub, dried them and set them back in their place, calling to their mother that she was going to find Hawk before heading out the door and into the sunshine.

Her mother's laughter and a cheerful, "Good luck!" followed her.

Standing still as silence just outside the shelter, she closed her eyes and concentrated without thinking or effort. "Where are you?"

Clearly, she heard a giggle in her mind.

"I'm not kidding around- mom told me to make sure you didn't get dirty this morning. Where are you?"

"Helping".

Sighing again, Fern thought to herself, "Well, that narrows it down to anywhere". She shook her head and looked around.

Opening her eyes, but depending on her mind- she studied the relative open space of the clearing…only the very tiniest of children could hide in the tidiness around the shelters, and he was small, but not that small.

She allowed her gaze to sift over each shelter in turn…all seemed in order- no diminutive figure floated up the vines like a shadow monkey. She then turned to the surrounding forest, but though there were endless places both to hide and to help there, it just didn't feel right. She was drawn to the goat pen off to one side.

Made of the same building materials as the human shelters, the goat house was just smaller and lacked glass in the windows. The fence around it was woven wattle, gathered by hand and hand-laced with both slender saplings and yards and yards of the thorny vines that were the bane of anyone trying to travel cross country- natural barbed wire. The fence mirrored all the other structures- meandering around trees and following the rise and fall of the land itself.

Inside the pen, Hawk sat snuggled up to a huge white dog and they were both intently supervising a newborn goatling still wet from being born, its little legs seemed to be made of jelly, but they were just trying to adjust from their recently aquatic lodgings.

Each time the little creature tried to stand up she collapsed again, smacked down repeatedly by gravity and insecurity.

Fern 'heard' her brother and knew both he and the dog were willing the little thing to get up, - stand up and gain strength.

"Up. Up. Up."

-flop-

"Ok. You're OK. Up. Up. Up."

-flop-

"Almost did it that time. Again. Up. Up. Up."

And the goatling gathered her legs under herself, and carefully unfolded them upward- first the back legs and then the front legs. She swayed back and forth in an invisible breeze of unfamiliarity. Balancing precariously on her tiny hooves, she tried one step, and then another. Gaining momentum she stumbled a step, walked a step then ran to her waiting mother.

Hawk and the dog both smiled.

Fern smiled back at them, walked over and plopped down beside them to watch the antics of the new little goat. She wasn't jealous of her brother's ability to 'talk' to the animals- everyone had unique gifts that were discovered early in life and encouraged. Growing up and becoming educated and productive members of the group involved expanding, honing and developing innate talents instead of hiding and suppressing them in an attempt to have everyone appear exactly the same as everyone else.

This trend against homogenization did not weaken society, as had previously been thought.

The more varied the group, the greater its autonomy, strength and ability to be able to draw whatever knowledge and skills necessary from within. Not that that meant isolation- everyone for miles around knew where the most skilled Healers, Craftspeople, Agrarians and Teachers were located- all knowledge was shared generously and freely, without demands or rancor.

When she wasn't supervising Hawk's excursions into the goat pen, down to the creek to commune with the tadpoles, perched on a branch to steady fledgling blue jays, under a brush pile to keep a hen company while her brood hatched, Fern spent her time building.

The entire area outside of their shelter was a maze of intricate and elegant roads, canals and bridges woven through each other in undulating graceful patterns, interspersed with tiny little shelters built to scale using pebbles, twigs and grass instead of rocks, logs and straw.

No one would've thought to admonish her to "clean that mess up" or to tell her she was "doing it wrong". Adults and other children alike complimented her on the good aspects of her creation and knew that she'd ask for advice when something just didn't seem right.

It's easy to ask for help when there's no fear of ridicule.

She didn't get frustrated or feel ashamed when she had an element that didn't work on the first (or tenth) attempt. She sat back and re-evaluated it and tried again. If she felt the need to ask for advice, she decided which adult (or child) to ask and they'd accommodate respectfully and seriously- giving their opinion without derision or direct interference.

Life was learning and no one thought of themselves as an expert in anything. Everyone had gifts and talents, yes. But there was always something new to learn from each and every person, and no one talent held more value than another.

Whenever she and Hawk decided the time was right, they'd apprentice to an adult with their gift in order to further develop their own skills. This mentor would nurture and encourage, share ways of doing and being that let the energy flow more easily and in a directed manner, and all the while listen to their pupil who would invariably teach them many things as well.

Hawk was already spending much of his time with their father, learning how to do more than 'feel' the animals. Equally important was gaining the practical knowledge to take the best care of them; not only because they depended on them for sustenance, but out of respect for them as other living creatures inhabiting the same planet as they themselves did, no better than them and no worse.

Darius in turn had learned from his own fathers, who had been very successful stockmen and willing teachers during the Destruction when agriculture was being completely overhauled; the entire domestic food chain re-thought by necessity rather than from whims and trends.

Lucas and Gerald had been advocates for small family farms several decades before that sort of knowledge became more than fashionable pastimes for people with leisure time and life-enhancing endeavors of the hard core remnants of the back-to-the-landers.

They'd met while abandoning their homes and lives-the winds of change were blowing in an incredibly intolerant and foreboding way. Headed out of the rural areas they'd been born into, both were mourning more than loss of familiarity and family- they were country boys through and through, and dreaded their assumed fate as residents of the urban jungle.

They became reluctant passengers on an unofficial underground railroad headed into the more forgiving larger urban areas.

One night they both happened to stop at the same place and struck up a conversation which hatched a plan and a future.

They inched as near to the social safety of a large city as they could- straddling precariously between urban and rural living. There they were able to buy up an entire subdivision that had been abandoned one house at a time by people suddenly unemployed as the corporations and manufacturers made deep cuts and laid off many employees.

When Lucas and Gerald approached the developer/mortgage holder with an offer that was a tiny fraction of the stated worth of the properties, the bank took it and ran- cleverly writing off the rest as an unfortunate loss of the trying economic times.

Tearing out every single upgrade and energy saving feature from the houses and donating them to folks who still needed them but couldn't afford them- furnaces, air conditioners, dish washers… they then scoured second hand stores and junk yards to retrofit them with screen windows, and wood stoves, and fans, were able to turn lawns and flower beds into vegetable gardens and orchards- planting vines and trees on sunny sides of the houses between the windows and the vegetables in an effort to counteract the mostly arbitrary way the houses were positioned on the land.

People came out from the cities and in from the rural areas to see, to learn, and to go home and replicate. Being even a little bit self-sufficient gave them more actual security than the largest arsenal or pantry of freeze-dried survival food, nurtured a sense of belonging to the earth which fed their souls, and encouraged community instead of the misguided isolation that armaments bred.

Lucas and Gerald had been scraping by not as well as some but better than others and loving what they were doing so it really didn't matter much.

There was enough money to pay their few bills and enough food to eat and they loved teaching others about living sustainably and lightly on the land practicing organic gardening, poultry and goat husbandry, and bee keeping. Folks came and stayed a weekend or a week in the comfortable redesigned homes and it was a pleasant, routine and quiet life, even after the Destruction began. Since they were already set up to run mostly without outside power or supplies, it made barely a ruffle in their days and nights.

During the initial confusion and frustrations of the Liberation, there were random instances of violence and looting, but even with their proximity to the large city Lucas and Gerald's obviously primitive little farm was passed by over and over again in favor of places that "looked prosperous"- the big fancy gated subdivisions and the huge ranches with the imposing and impressive gates.

So life went on for them pretty much as planned.

And with the extra houses, they were yet another safe stop for other travelers.

When news of Gerald's sister's death reached them, it was accompanied by Darius- barely 2 years old, emaciated and scared to death.

The official who deposited Darius and his meager belongings at their doorstep informed them that Cat (short for Catherine) had died of malnutrition in an indigent hospital still nursing Darius- trying to sustain her son.

Her husband had abandoned them rather than face them every day knowing he could not provide for them, and she had had neither money nor means to travel to her brother and no way to contact him; during those times phone service was non-existent or very expensive and mail service almost as bad.

It was an odd yet unsurprising state of affairs that the only way for Cat to receive help to send her son to her brother was for her to die. Delivering orphans to next of kin was one of the only grudging acts of charity the government still adhered to, and they only did that because the cost of running orphanages was considered an extravagant expense.

Lucas and Gerald took turns holding Darius, who wasn't walking or talking yet, and feeding him anything he wanted on demand. Fresh fruits and vegetables, fresh milk from the goats, eggs, and toast with honey- the boy seemed to blossom overnight and day by day grew stronger and more active.

Within 6 months he wasn't walking- he was running. And he wasn't merely talking- he was talking in full sentences. Gerald saw his sister in Darius' face and eyes and his heart broke and swelled with love simultaneously every time he looked at the boy.

Darius was a good son and helped anywhere he was asked to or was needed, but his true love was always the livestock. He had a way with them that was almost spooky to people who've never seen the bond between certain people and animals.

The farm and his fathers and their life together were all that mattered to Darius. He was pleasant and cheerful to those who came through- people who knew they needed to learn how to grow their own food…and in short order, as well as travelers needing somewhere to stay on their road from a home lost to a home yet to be found.

Jose and Maria was one such couple. The farm was full of people that weekend and all the guest houses were occupied. Luckily there was a small loft apartment above the barn- hardly ever used because the running water and bathroom were downstairs- just a living area and sleeping nook were up in the loft. The couple was grateful to get it and Maria said it didn't matter that she was very pregnant- the steps would do her good as she was a little bit overdue and was over-ready to have her child.

Baby Jesse was born there in the loft and the healer Eliza was summoned to attend the birth. She brought her daughter Hope to assist her as she always did. Hope was only a year younger than Darius.

Hope's first encounter with Darius was almost disastrous. One of the goats had sprung the gate latch and ventured into the barn- the extra activity and strange noises from the loft intrigued her. She'd found a basket at the bottom of the stairs that had a baby blanket in it and had tested it for flavor and found it to be palatable. When Hope came down the steps for a glass of water for the new mother she was infuriated to find the goat working a hole in the corner of the blanket- not an easy feat since goats have only front teeth and molars, but she was a dedicated goat and of a singular mind when she had a self-appointed project.

Darius came running at the torrent of expletives that was streaming out of the barn- each one sharply barbed and aimed at his beloved livestock. The goat was clearly and rightly terrified- Hope had on hand a few, just a few, extra blankets for the babies of travelers, and she was not amused at the fate of this one.

It took only a moment for Darius to grab the collar of the offending nanny and usher her back into the fenced enclosure, closing the gate securely behind her. He then turned on the girl, hands outstretched and low, quiet voice, easy movements- the same way he'd approach any other wild and angry creature. "Here, now- it's ok- she didn't do any harm that can't be fixed- she was only curious and the flowers on that blanket look more real than the ones in the meadow…"

Hope's left eyebrow came up and she tried very hard to remain livid.

She couldn't do it.

He was so charming and sincere she was forced to smile.

They examined the blanket together to assess the damage. Only one tiny bite had been managed in the folded corner and when it was opened up…there was a perfect little (goat spittle soaked) heart.

How could a beginning like that bode anything less than magical endings?

Hope and Darius were the generation that balanced on the edge of what was left of the old ways. The birth of their children tipped them fully into the new and they never looked back. The death of the old society was so ugly and ignoble that there was nothing there they wanted to cling to.

So Hawk was already apprenticed to his father to sharpen and hone his gift of working with animals, and they both spent days on end at the farm of the grandfathers, who doted on Hawk as they had on Darius.

This left Fern plenty of time to work out the many ideas that organized themselves in her head, bringing them to life with her hands and seeing if what she saw in her mind's eye would work when pummeled by wind and rain, gently pressured by occupation and gravity.

There was a Builder several days to the other side of Unity who had already paid a visit to Fern, admiring the work she'd done, tilting her head at some of the minor adjustments the girl had made to existing building techniques and chuckling. "Nice! Very nice- why didn't I think of that?" she said, and then she asked Fern to consider coming to build with her whenever she felt ready.

Parents and grandparents would, of course be consulted in any big decision like moving to a different place, but so would Hawk and the younger family members- everyone's opinion held equal importance and the deciding vote was always with the person directly affected, no matter if they were eight years old, or eighty.

Fern knew what her gifts were, and when the time came, she'd know when and where to go. In the meantime, her days were spent learning and reading, creating and planning. In her head she saw shapes and angles, buildings and roads, whether her eyes were open or closed, whether she was awake or asleep.

She woke with a startle when the big white dog sneezed, then licked her face apologetically. She'd been watching the goatling with her brother and had just closed her eyes for a minute…she thought. But now the sun was high in the sky, the baby goatling dry and fluffy, nursing contentedly.

And Hawk was gone.

Of course.

Fern stretched and yawned, patted the big dog on the head and stood up; brushing the clean straw from her pants and the images of a bridge she wanted to build from her thoughts. Shaking her head in consternation mixed with amusement, Fern closed her eyes and thought, *"Where are you NOW?"*

"Helping".

"Well, help yourself home- it's almost time for Thanksgiving meal and if we're not there on time, we'll miss the reading of the story".

The dog smiled and its tail fanned in affection and farewell as Fern made her way out of the goat pen and headed to the celebration.

In the distance, she heard her great-grandmother's voice and could see the other children gathered around her, glancing furtively and curiously at the three stones gathered up in netting and tied with a twine bow in the center of the huge table.

Crispin was smiling and telling the tiniest children to wait for the story and then they'd know the secret of the stones. The older children grinned conspiratorially- they already knew but they'd never spoil it for the younger ones.

Completely out of the blue, new building plans came into Fern's head and she knew she'd have to disassemble a large part of her creation. Far from upsetting her, she accepted that calmly, knowing that de-struction is every bit as important as con-struction.

Destruction 2065- Hope

Getting used to the silence was the hardest thing of all.

It rang in their ears, throbbed through their veins, weighed them down physically till they ducked and instinctively crouched against it.

Eliza caught herself, straightened up, and stood taller, noting that Hope did the same; shadowlike.

Sighing inwardly, Eliza wondered if she'd ever be able to relax enough to stand without stooping and sleep without startling.

Eight years. It had been eight years since the Destruction began.

What a mess.

Eliza hugged Hope, brushed the hair from her daughter's face with her tired fingers and said, "Thank you for your help, darling- I think I can take it from here".

She watched Hope till she disappeared around the corner and saw with a small spark of happiness that when out of her orbit, Hope traveled fully upright and unaffected by the weight of the silence.

And why not?

Hope had known nothing else.

Eliza turned back to the woman on the bed who was lost in a world of her own- inhabited by only herself and the tiny new person residing in the crook of her arm- less than a foot away from where he'd been living for the last twelve months, but now in an entirely different world- as different as being on another planet.

Another birth. More importantly, another healthy birth.

While she cleaned up the room, Eliza thought back eight years.

The entire country had been in labor pains with the Liberation- fighting each other, fighting themselves, starting slowly and almost imperceptibly then building over the years to that very last moment when everything came to a sudden and violent simultaneous ending and beginning and Eliza remembered it because that's the very moment

Hope was born.

Breathing shallowly, so the air didn't burn her lungs quite so badly, Hope walked the short distance from where she had helped her mother with this last birth to their own house.

Hope knew that the air hadn't always burned; the breeze hadn't always been flocks of invisible acidic knives cutting coldly through clothing. Water had once been safe to drink without boiling, filtering through layers of sand and charcoal and then steeped with sachets of antibacterial plants.

None of that had been caused by the events of the Liberation, of course.

The environment had been altered by the heady days of unfettered capitalism- during the time of the Reclamation all environmental safety regulations had been repealed in the same fevered rush as anything else that smacked of "socialism" or "liberalism". Hauled out into the open, tarred, feathered and then drowned in the bathtub with all social programs, all laws that infringed on the imagined rights of a small and violent segment of the population- history repeated itself yet again and the Will of the Powerful Few was foisted on the Downtrodden Many- causing untold unnecessary death and destruction in the name of Freedom.

No, the air and water had been sacrificed before the Liberation. It was just one more way they had to adjust and adapt- mentally and physically- in the face of something too big to fix, a road traveled too far to come back from.

One of the dubious benefits of falling off of a cliff is being able to dismiss outright any resolution that starts with, "First- before falling…"

Sheri Dixon

Being compelled to only look ahead makes focusing easier.

Hope turned one final corner and skipped up the stairs to their house, admiring the tough little annuals and perennials growing cheerfully on either side of the steps. She remembered her parents telling her as they planted them years ago, "Herbs thrive in conditions other plants run away from", and they all laughed at the vision of flowers pulling up roots and scampering away, leaving a trail of soil behind them.

Opening the door, she smiled as she was met with the warm fresh aroma of both food and the simmering herbs in the kettle. The food would be delicious because Griffin was an excellent cook, and the herbs allowed them to breathe deeply inside the house.

The Thanksgiving dinner was as traditional as possible within the restricted availability of foodstuffs. Locally raised chicken was cooked with vegetables and liberally laced with herbs that both promoted immune function and had antibacterial qualities- basil, rosemary, thyme; so many that took the place of mere salt which was difficult to come by and did nothing for a body of its own accord.

Every meal was flavored and brightened with peppers, onions and garlic- age old poor mans' defense against disease.

Honey took the place of refined sugar and added its own benefits to their evolving lungs and digestive tracts.

"Need any help, dad?" Hope asked.

Griffin grinned at her with a twinkle in his eyes and said, "Anything I could ask you to do would be gravy next to helping your mother deliver another baby…how about making the gravy?"

"Already? Isn't it too early yet? Mom won't be home for another hour, at least. Now that I know the new baby is a boy, I'd like to finish the blanket I was making for him".

Griffin made an elaborate show of thinking this request over, frowning in deep thought. He looked at the clock with serious exaggeration, peeked at the cooking food- tasting here, sniffing there, even listening…which brought the barely-contained giggles bursting out of Hope.

Finally he proclaimed, "I deem your request reasonable, and your motives pure. Proceed as requested".

Giving her dad a quick hug, Hope disappeared into the back of the house where her sewing things were gathered.

Griffin looked after her adoringly. She looked just like her mother, just like her mother without the worry and care that now hung shroud like around her shoulders.

Just like her mother when he had first seen her- as beautiful as Eliza was, she was even more beautiful angry with her cheeks flushed and her eyes blazing. And she was very, very angry when Griffin first met her.

He had been minding his own business- just leaving work for the day and like most days there was a line of protestors outside the lab. All the employees were so used to seeing the signs and banners that the only time they'd even stop to take note is if they walked out the door and there was no one there at all. But that hadn't happened in months.

Something was going wrong.

Griffin had always considered himself moderately brilliant and absolutely ethical.

He'd skated through college on a fistful of well-earned scholarships and been plucked straight out of the college lab and into the corporate lab of HemoPlas, all on the coat tail of his baby, his discovery, his project- a little doo-hickie that looked like that thing in the junk drawer that no one claims or is able to identify, but this one allowed medical staff to draw blood from donors with less hassle (for them) and less pain (for the donors).

In this day and age where getting a job at all, much less a job in your chosen field was almost unheard of, Griffin snapped at the offer and swallowed the hook. His family and friends were thrilled with his luck and proud of his genius.

The first year at HemoPlas was busy and blurred and he spent so much time concentrating on the technical process that he paid almost no attention to the donors themselves. He wasn't unfeeling or uninterested; like many specialists, Griffin was so focused on making sure his little bit of the whole was perfect, he just never looked at anything else, assuming all the other technicians and doctors were as meticulous as he was.

He did notice the protestors outside, lining the sidewalk to the staff parking lot. He saw the signs and absentmindedly read them, like noting cracks in the cement or squirrels in the trees.

"HUMAN RIGHTS NOT CORPORATE MIGHT"

"HEMOPLAS- MONEY TO DIE FOR"

"FIRST, DO NO HARM"

"YOU MAKE ME LOOK SO GOOD- DRACULA"

It was that last sign that make him stop and listen. The protestors were chanting as the employees walked to their cars- "Vampires! Vampires! Vampires!"

Griffin slept fitfully that night.

The next day he looked at the donors- really looked at them.

And he was shocked.

All day long, they filed in to give blood and plasma, although they were paid and paid well, especially for those with the less common blood types so it really wasn't a donation at all.

That's where the problem was.

The economy had continued its downward spiral. Money was scarce and unemployment was high. People still got sick, still needed surgery, still were in car wrecks and did things that caused them to need transfusions.

The number of work-related accidents rose as people worked longer hours for less pay and the corporations gutted the unions and safety standards. Manufacturing and agricultural injuries skyrocketed- all of them messy and all requiring blood. Gallons of blood.

Women were once again driven to seek back alley abortions as the theocracy tightened its grip and not only were the safe medical options eliminated, but contraceptives were made illegal and "abstinence only" was the one single birth control method taught in schools.

In the current economy, how was a family to feed multiple mouths? Women literally risked their lives to do the responsible thing for their families- and those who suffered the common complications needed antibiotics for infection, and blood. Gallons of blood.

Many weren't that lucky. Many died.

There were rumors that the rising single car/single occupant accidents were actually suicides, but no one said it out loud, and there were never notes left.

Life insurance doesn't pay on suicide. Those lucky enough to have life insurance were painfully aware that they were worth more dead than alive.

Those who miscalculated trajectory or veered at the last moment and didn't die needed blood. Gallons of blood.

Of course there was a limit to how often a person could donate, and careful records were kept on file. But between the increased need for their product and the increased desperation of their donors, the people in the front office had been told to bend the rules…just a tad. Surely double donations wouldn't hurt anyone much, and the hospitals were depending almost solely on them- the day of the volunteer blood drives had gone the way of other charities. No one had spare time, or money, or generosity.

Why give away something you could be paid for?

When folks in the surrounding area had inexplicably started passing out in random places- at work, in their homes, in church- they were rushed to the hospital and found to be dangerously anemic. It took several months of guess work and conjecture, tracing backwards to a common denominator to find the link.

Because these weren't homeless hobos- they WERE working and had families. Was it something in the air? A mosquito-borne disease? A rogue germ?

No, nothing worthy of an adventure film or mystery book.

It was the high expenses and low wages combining to make even basic survival very difficult for everyone except those at the tippy top of the Free Market Pyramid, and Griffin realized sickeningly that he WAS a vampire- unwitting, but a vampire all the same. He was able to be very successful and financially secure by literally and physically sucking people dry.

For the next few days Griffin really saw the endless parade of donors- now that he'd started seeing, he couldn't stop.

He looked beyond their arm with the needle and other apparatus perfectly in place.

Their eyes were wells of sadness, their shoulders heavy with worry, they each and every one of them grasped a thin cloak of dignity that inadequately covered their core of resignation and defeat.

At the end of the third day he demanded a meeting with the owner of HemaPlas.

Sitting in the quiet elegance of the executive suite, Griffin listened to the words of calm bureaucratic reason- every donor read and signed a release form stating the dangers of too many donations too often. They were fully informed and made their own decisions. Free market…supply and demand…yada…yada…yada.

The faces of the people swam in front of his mind's eye as he listened- bodies floating in a fetid ocean of corporate-speak waves, dashed and broken on a reef of impersonal greed.

Griffin nodded silently and left the plush cocoon of the top floor. He gathered his personal things- he was surprised how few 'personal things' he had in his desk. His entire life up to that point had been clean, and straightforward, and uncomplicated, and he left the building.

That life was over.

The next morning he parked his company car in the parking lot, left the keys in it and walked over to the line of protestors and there she was- wrapped in a worn yet brilliantly colored shawl, brandishing her sign defiantly, as different from the people he'd seen the day before as could be and still be the same species. They were defeated, hopeless. She was alive, filled with fire. And really, really pissed off.

She glared at him and for a split second he thought she just might spit at him or deck him with her sign. Instead she just eyed him suspiciously and asked, "Well?"

"I, ummm…do you happen to have a spare sign? And I'm going to need a ride home tonight".

Eliza liked to tell people that she'd made a horrible mistake. That she'd given him a ride home and it was the beginning of the end. He was like a fed cat, and she just couldn't get rid of him after that. Griffin never failed to just grin and shrug.

He wondered yet again at the miracle of Hope's birth- the timing of it making all the difference in the world. Eliza had been well-nourished during her pregnancy, and Hope had breastfed for the first few years of her life- Eliza's milk providing immunities and nutrition not found elsewhere during the first years of the Destruction.

Griffin had watched Eliza suffer- both physically and mentally during those years. As a healer, she could barely stand to see other children- those who were toddlers when it all began- wither and sicken and die. She ministered to them as she could but of course in those early days when the air was almost solid with toxins and the food and water questionable at best it was grasping at straws and hoping for miracles and nothing more.

The faces of those other mothers would haunt her forever, imploring her to do something, anything to make it right and save their children and all she had were cures that were no longer viable, experiments that were not yet tested, grasping at straws, hoping for miracles and nothing more.

Half a decade of children was lost, and another half a decade more would be born heartbreakingly ill-equipped to survive, if they were even conceived.

The air was too foul, the food too scarce and too affected by the vile conditions of the water. Tainted not enough to kill an adult, but enough to kill a child and to cross a mother's bloodstream and disrupt the peculiar miracle that is billions of single cells all coordinating to become a single living creature.

As if the silence caused by everything turning off at once and forever weren't enough, that was compounded by the silence of human loss- an entire decade without infants' cries or toddlers laughing.

Griffin did what he could to shield Eliza from the horrors of her calling- helping woman after woman give birth to empty arms and endless tears. But now, finally, just as the country was healing after the insult of Destruction, everything alive was altering, adapting, evolving- amazing for such a short period of time until Earth's long history is observed on large and small scales.

Damage done cannot be undone, but it can scar over, new life springs from death and craters fill with blooms, flowers in the ashes.

The Earth heals Herself in spite of Her parasites, not because of them.

The last three years had brought babies back into the human family. Smaller, darker, more sinewy and less cherubic, these infants took almost a full year before birth- those extra few months inside giving them the edge they needed to survive outside- the air was still sharp, the food plants and animals still evolving as well to adjust to the new atmosphere and water.

Hope had been helping her mother for two years now. That's how long she'd been making protective blankets for the babies once they were born.

Their home had been an abandoned fabric shop before the destruction and there were bolts and bolts of fabric, spools and spools of thread, all the accoutrements of a seamstress even though Eliza and Griffin had no use for any of it. They had chosen this building for its proximity to the town square and for its solid old countenance- built of rock it only needed new shutters and some roof patching to be habitable.

They thought it was perhaps only chance that brought them to this place, but once they realized Hope's gift with a needle and thread they knew better.

When Hope was four she discovered the fabric, and spent hours arranging and rearranging bolts according to color, pattern, and texture.

When Hope was five she was allowed a blunt-tipped scissors and she started cutting out squares of material and piecing together quilts in patterns both intricate and bold, subtle and cheerful.

When Hope was six she started sewing them together under the willing guidance of her grandmother Crispin, who knew the basics of sewing and recognized a Gift when she saw it.

At seven, Hope's needle and thread took on a life of their own, not only sewing the patches together with tiny precise stitches, but also meandering across the quilts in a multi-colored litany of vines, flowers, trees, feathers…

Today she curled up with the soft fleece blanket she'd been working on since helping her mother with this particular pregnancy- it was done in blues and greens soft and calm as the surface of a pond and after seeing the deep violet eyes of the new baby, she knew he'd have an affinity for water and her needle and thread swam fishes all across the surface of the blanket, with one little turtle up in the corner.

Her mind wandered as her fingers finished up the quilt she'd deliver tomorrow.

She thought about the new baby- one of many now that were being born healthy and strong. It seemed strange to her- all these new little people. There were adults, teens, a few precious children Hope's age, then nothing at all till the last few years.

With every stitch she willed strength and happiness into the blanket that would surround the new baby with warmth. Every single baby in town had a similar blanket made by her- in all different colors and patterns, each as unique as the children they swaddled.

It seemed to her that the adults and teens were always a little sad, a little shell-shocked, and a little less…alive than Life called for. As though they were afraid to smile and be happy; what they'd lost when the Destruction began was always near the surface to remind them that 'then' was better than 'now', and they dreaded even what they had now would be taken from them if they forgot to be afraid- even for a minute.

Hope couldn't remember 'before'.

She was born into the sudden silence of cataclysmic change.

Her parents told her the story of her birth- how Eliza had labored and Griffin had stood by her and at the exact moment Hope had been born there was an earthquakingly, blindingly, breathtakingly silent "WHOOSH" as the entire web of running, humming mechanism of the country seemed to inhale without exhaling, tick without tocking, and the world as they knew it was gone.

They said they weren't even aware of it for the first few moments- they were too busy realizing that they had gone from being a couple to a family in the blink of an eye.

Eliza had cried out mightily with the final contraction- the one that brought Hope into the world, and they hadn't heard or felt anything else except their own personal world tipping on its axis. It took some minutes of three pairs of eyes locked onto each other in a first wave of bonding before they realized that they were also hearing three heartbeats, three sets of lungs…and nothing else.

The lights in the birthing room had gone out; only the daylight filtered in, foggy and discolored as always.

Even though their town was small and sparsely populated, Eliza and Griffin knew they needed to go- take their newborn daughter and go as quickly and as far as they could from whatever had just occurred.

Covering their mouths and noses and loosely wrapping a sheet completely over Hope in an instinctive gesture of "just in case", they left the small hospital along with everyone else who had been there and they got into their car.

The silence was deafening and the sound of the engine starting up roared in their ears.

None of the traffic lights worked. The telephones had all been turned off, as had apparently the entire world.

Turned off.

The silence thicker than the fog, they breathed timidly through the cloth over their faces- the mere sound of a deep breath suddenly aggressive and invasive, and they drove slowly. Away. They drove away.

Everyone was driving as in a trance- whispering to each other, not used to the quiet of a world without machinery noise- humming, running, rumbling, buzzing the background of their lives.

They drove as night fell and the evening fog rolled in, as it did every day. Both seemed suddenly of a menacing and unnatural nature.

The air smelled metallic, felt electrical. The fog burned their eyes and froze on their eyelashes. Both Griffin and Eliza had grown up in the polluted atmosphere, but somehow it had been cushioned and masked by the constant vibration and hum of their mechanized world.

Eliza started to cry, tears freezing on her cheeks even though it was not winter. They'd been so close.

So close to bringing the world around to a better future, not just for the very wealthy, but for everyone. They had been sure that their child would be born into the new world, and they were right.

And heartbreakingly wrong.

The ensuing years had brought some understanding of what had happened- the corporations knew of the coming sanctions, knew their time in charge of the soon-to-be former greatest country on Earth was coming to an ungraceful and cheerless end in just a matter of months, and having taken all there was to take both in human labor and environmental plunder from the country anyway, in a final act of "No hard feelings- it's only good business", the ruling class had simply and actually pulled the plug on the nation- all utilities, gasoline, communications, everything all at once and forever.

They'd seen the writing on the wall and had taken themselves and their families to a remote area overseas that had been stocked and set up for just such an eventuality. Of course never in their wildest dreams had they thought it would be the rest of the nations who would instigate such a drastic move- they'd always assumed the peasants would do something…violent and uncivilized.

But it hadn't happened that way at all.

Sheri Dixon

The peasants had used skills, education, diplomacy and old-fashioned boycotts, lawsuits, elections, organizing and protesting to niggle and agitate the elite like relentless gnats, not necessarily preventing them from doing what they wanted to, but making it less than easy, not as effortless as they'd like.

It was extremely unfair and maddening, but not incredibly damaging.

What did make a huge difference was being told that unless the government changed their ways- ways that were steeped in oil and dominance and a too-big-to-stop-feeding war industry along with a totally failed economic structure, that the US would be deemed persona non grata at the table of every civilized government in the world.

There was no way to change any of that easily and in their favor.

So they'd pulled the plug and that had set a whole chain of nasty reactions in action.
From the meltdown of nuclear reactors to the death of millions of livestock in feed lots and the death of billions of plants without the chemicals they needed to survive, and the all-encompassing shut down of both luxuries and necessities for those left behind-food deliveries and storage, water, heat, light, communications- the 100 wealthiest families in the country, none of whom had never had their photos in a newspaper or had their name uttered by anyone as

Someone Important- quietly and thoughtlessly cast the Space Age mightiest nation on earth back into the Stone Age and whisked off to their hideaway.

The only "boots on the ground" attack they made was not on the people en masse and not on the roads or buildings or any of those other warlike targets.

Thirty days before abandoning the country, there were sudden mysterious deaths in unlikely places- elementary schools, colleges, libraries. People were perplexed and a little worried since there seemed to be no correlation between the deaths.

The week before they switched everything off a news bulletin pierced the airwaves- a mold had been discovered and isolated. The atmospheric conditions of the previous year had caused the entire country to be just a bit more humid than normal (according to the colorful charts they produced) and that had spawned a mutated mold that enjoyed a symbiotic relationship with the dust mites that were indigenous to printing paper.

Anyone coming into contact with the mold was susceptible to inhaling it and becoming sick or worse.

The CDC was ordered to set fire to all public libraries, private libraries, museums, and book stores. The owners and caretakers of these locations were informed they'd be financially compensated for their loss and told not to fret since all that information was on computers now anyway.

Sheri Dixon

There was mostly compliance, but some of the librarians were skeptical and refused the orders. They refused to leave their books and their libraries-chaining themselves to the bookcases. They were given three warnings and then the libraries were set aflame with the librarians inside- this was the New America where an individual's choice to die with their books was to be respected and admired.

Those who had ordered the incinerations slept with clear consciences secure in that knowledge and absolutely sure that anything that could paint them in a bad light in the stark black and white of the written word had vanished.

Their plan was to wait for the world's economy to rebound on its own and the silly sanctions to be lifted. By that time the environment would have renewed itself with a fresh supply of resources.

They'd regroup and come back with a vengeance disguised as being the new saviors of a primitive culture. It was the perfect plan.

Unfortunately, the filters in their transport planes' air ducts were growing a mutated mold that enjoyed a symbiotic relationship with the dust mites that were indigenous to the suitcases filled with paper money they'd brought with them in a fit of rare capitalist sentimentality. Anyone coming into contact with the mold was susceptible to inhaling it and becoming sick or worse.

The symptoms were identical to any number of nasty intestinal viruses and before they realized what the source of their distress was and could call in medical help they all died a horribly embarrassing death.

Proving definitively that you may be able to take it with you, but you really shouldn't.

Meanwhile, back in the country they'd destroyed and then abandoned, those who had been working towards a better and more sustainable world already had the mindset of Community in place and had been practicing many forms of food and shelter independence.

They knew they had to work together and pool knowledge and resources if they were to understand what the toxins were in the air and water and how to counteract them with a minimum of sickness and death, and how to alter and step up food production now that factory farming and agri-business were suddenly a thing of the past.

To be sure, most of the people had been too busy just surviving to have any time for recreational pastimes like following the news, or paying attention to politics, and when everything just...stopped, they didn't quite know what to do.

A great percentage talked to their neighbors-sometimes for the first time ever, and in the void left by mass communications they spun reality scenarios ranging from a far-away super storm, to a terrorist act, to the vengeful hand of the lord.

So their responses ranged from literally circling their wagons in preparation for the arrival of terrorist armies, to packing their bibles and awaiting the sure coming of the Rapture, but most just decided to make the best of things till everything came back on again.

Some even went into work till their cars ran out of gas for the commute, sitting in their dark offices and staring at their black computer screens all day. After all, a person is only allowed so many days off without being fired for absenteeism.

Those who had been hoarding weapons for a coming apocalypse were sorely disappointed when they realized that good people were *not* driven instantly to lives of wanton crime, and they grumbled into their bullet-proof vests whenever anyone mentioned how wonderful it was to see people working together.

As is always the case whenever there's a disruption in society for any reason, the very young and the very old were most adversely affected. Toddlers' little tummies couldn't adapt quickly enough and they lacked the body mass to cope. Pregnant women lost their babies. Old people faded away without their medications and in the face of the toxins forced on already weak immune systems.

But the people persevered. They continued as they had started to pull together instead of apart and their new world took shape, albeit in a much different process than they had envisioned.

There were still pockets of "might makes right" and "live by the sword" renegades here and there, however they were just as sick and hungry and stranded as anyone else and mostly spent the first months being pissed off and shooting up all their ammunition at each other since they didn't trust anyone, ever; even members of their own enclaves.

Those who straggled out and back into society were shamed, then guarded as they were taught to act in a civil manner in a civil society. Banishment awaited anyone who was a sociopath, and that way lay starvation or death at the hands of whoever had survived in their old haunts. Most became civil.

History shows over and over that while an evil mindset can have power for a short time, humans are social animals and the species will not tolerate it for long.

Rugged individualists who spurn community end up crazy or dead- we need each other not just to survive, but to live.

Vengeful gods and armed solutions only cripple civilization by dividing people who would otherwise be working together and delay peace by continuing a violent agenda.

The clock in the living room struck the hour. It was an old wind-up clock and Griffin had looked at the sun and guessed at the time when they brought it home and set it. Time was mostly immaterial now, but it added a comforting touch to their little house-its very own heartbeat.

The tired sun slipped under the incoming evening fog and the tattered little town shifted uneasily into the coming night.

Hope's fingers stitched of their own accord and the little fishes streamed across the fabric leaving ripples in the folds of the fleece and dove around the edge of the material with a flip of their jewel-toned tails, leaving the little turtle in the corner looking after them, astonished.

It was finished.

She carefully folded it and set it aside, then went into the kitchen and washed up, ready to help her dad finish the Thanksgiving dinner, arriving just as Griffin gently placed the three little stones wrapped in netting and tied with a twine bow into the broth.

Her mother had sent word that they were to start the reading of the story without her- she'd be there before it finished and then dinner wouldn't be too late- both Eliza and Hope were exhausted from helping with the birth and bed sounded so good to them.

True to her word, Eliza quietly opened the door, crossed the room and cozied in between Griffin and Hope, in time for the second half of the Thanksgiving Story-

Stone soup? That would be something to know about.

"First, we'll need a large iron pot," the old woman said.

The peasants brought the largest pot they could find. How else to cook enough?

"That's none too large," said the old woman. "But it will do. And now, water to fill it and a fire to heat it."

It took many buckets of water to fill the pot. A fire was built on the village square and the pot was set to boil.

"And now, if you please, three round, smooth stones."

Those were easy enough to find.

The peasants' eyes grew round as they watched the old woman drop the stones into the pot.

"Any soup needs salt and pepper," said the old woman, as she began to stir.

Children ran to fetch salt and pepper.

"Stones like these generally make good soup. But oh, if there were carrots, it would be much better."

"Why, I think I have a carrot or two," said Francoise, and off she ran.

She came back with her apron fill of carrots from the bin beneath the red quilt.

"A good stone soup should have cabbage," said the old woman as she sliced the carrots into the pot. "But no use asking for what you don't have."

"I think I could find a cabbage somewhere," said Marie and she hurried home. Back she came with three cabbages from the cupboard under the bed.

"If we only had a bit of beef and a few potatoes, this soup would be good enough for a rich man's table"

The peasants thought that over. They remembered their potatoes and the sides of beef hanging in the cellars. They ran to fetch them.

A rich man's soup – and all from a few stones. It seemed like magic!

"Ah," sighed the old woman as she stirred in the beef and potatoes, "if we only had a little barley and a cup of milk! This would be fit for the king himself. Indeed he asked for just such a soup when last he dined with me."

The peasants looked at each other. This old woman had entertained the king! Well!

"But – no use asking for what you don't have," the old woman shrugged.

The peasants brought their barley from the lofts; they brought their milk from the wells. The old woman stirred the barley and milk into the steaming broth while the peasants stared.

At last the soup was ready.

"All of you shall taste," the old woman said. "But first a table must be set."

Great tables were placed in the square. And all around were lighted torches.

Such a soup! How good it smelled! Truly fit for a king.

But then the peasants asked themselves, "Would not such a soup require bread – and a roast – and cider?" Soon a banquet was spread and everyone sat down to eat.

Never had there been such a feast. Never had the peasants tasted such soup. And fancy, made from stones!

They ate and drank and ate and drank. And after that they danced.

They danced and sang far into the night.

At last they were tired. Then the old woman asked, "Is there not a loft where I could sleep?"

"Let such a wise and splendid lady sleep in a loft? Indeed! You must have the best bed in the village."

So the old woman slept in the mayor's house.

In the morning, the whole village gathered in the square to give her a send-off.

"Many thanks for what you have taught us," the peasants said to the old woman. "We shall never go hungry, now that we know how to make soup from stones."

"Oh, it's all in knowing how," said the old woman, and off she went down the road, chuckling to herself.

As if on cue, all together they said, "And they lived happily ever after".

Hope looked from her mother to her father and back and smiled.

There were babies in the world. Healthy babies.

Society was adapting, evolving, growing in a healthy manner out of the sickly ashes of the Destruction.

Three sets of eyes locked onto each other as they had eight years before- Griffin's filled with calm determination, Eliza's with quiet elation, and Hope's with unadulterated liberation.

Liberation 2040- Eliza

"...with justice and liberty for all"

were the words above the door to the Sanctuary. Eliza read them silently to herself every day when she and her family walked under them- her parents Crispin and Gabriel, her older sister Jane, and herself.

The Sanctuary was just that, in several different ways.

It had been a church before the beginning of the Liberation and the words over the door had been carved in marble to last many lifetimes- "Believe in the One True God". That mantle piece had been pummeled by many hands hammering at it in defiance and it broke off gracelessly and smashed into shards on the floor, the words and the stone equally inflexible and brittle.

The new banner was woven of natural fibers and painted with earthen dyes and draped beautifully over the gaping and never-healing wound left behind. It would not last forever- it would need to be replaced every so often, but that's the way of living things, of life.

Life is evaluation, evolution, change.

Crispin and Gabriel had designated the Sanctuary as the community gathering place after its former inhabitants deserted it for their new home which was aptly named The Fortress, some ways out of town in a supposedly undisclosed location.

The Fortress was a wonderment of cement block buildings- almost windowless but for the sniper holes squinting suspiciously at the outside world and almost adornment-free but for the lightning rod cross at the peak of the main building, reminding the residents of their happy and joyous reward after their troubled time in this plain of sorrow ended. Inside there was rumored to be years and years of freeze dried and canned foodstuffs next to the hundreds of thousands of rounds of ammo to match the hundreds of different weapons.

Everything was painted a matte camo pattern and there was a bewildering maze of paths to it guarded by dour men and women in bunkers who barked out passwords straight from the scriptures.

Of course everyone in town knew right where it was- fact was no one bothered them at The Fortress because no one wanted to, not because they were so well hidden and defended.

But no one had a mean enough streak to tell them that.

They figured spending their days and nights locked in The Fortress with each other was punishment enough for any real or imagined sins the inhabitants had perpetrated.

The country was almost completely polarized now since the Patriot Party was firmly entrenched in both houses and the White House. Thanks to the long-ago ruling of Citizens United that gave carte blanche to the corporations to run the nation, the clever gerrymandering of voting districts to guarantee the election results and the decades-long marketing to the very people they were destroying there were still elections but they were mostly useless.

The new government had been steamrolled into the capitol on the shoulders of the anti-regulation gun owners who had twisted the 2nd Amendment to justify what they wanted, the fundamental Christians who had twisted the 1st Amendment to justify what *they* wanted, and the corporations who were amused and bemused that no matter how many decades passed with them taking all the money for themselves and leaving precious little for the vast majority of workers all they still had to do was put a flag and an eagle on their products and tell people the recovery was just around the corner and they not only bought the products but defended the corporations vehemently-calling anyone not walking in lock-step with them everything from Communists to Fascists to Marxists to just plain ol' traitors.

Subtly at first, then more obviously businesses, churches, entire neighborhoods shifted as America ceased to be the Melting Pot of the world and all its ingredients separated like oil and vinegar.

Intolerance ruled the day, suspicion ruled the night.

The Patriot Party had promised jobs, had promised money, had promised that everyone who was a 'hard worker' would be rewarded with a perfect America as remembered through the lenses of television cameras and the filter of convenience. That idyllic America that consisted of no poor people, no sickness, where the good guy always shot the bad guy and then went home with the pretty girl.

In reality, what they delivered was economic disaster both at home and abroad as the rest of the world became leery of doing business with an America that was reckless with its resources- human, monetary and environmental. The creed of American Exceptionalism became an empty caricature of liberty and success.

American food was no longer exported- no one would import it for the genetic engineering and the poisons and hormones used in it. Everywhere else considered it toxic.

American products were no longer exported- because there were no longer strong unions and safety regulations the items were shoddy at best, deadly at worst.

America was still free to import, of course, but it was horrendously expensive thanks to American banking practices. The Patriots believed that Capitalism works best when it's allowed total freedom, and now the dollar was virtually worthless.

The America that had been a beacon of hope and leadership to the world was now isolated, marginalized, of no consequence.

The Grand Experiment was over, and the world issued a collective sigh of disappointment and relief.

Of course nothing lasts forever, but the hope was always that their society would continue to evolve, not devolve. Most other places- Europe, Russia, China were all centuries older than America and had survived their share of upheaval and re-building and knew it was just a part of Being.

This was America's first brush with that reality and they were fighting it tooth and nail, so certain they could go on without changing when history clearly showed that nothing goes on forever unchanged. Change is inevitable and should be a time of growth and renewal.

America would have none of that.

The rest of the world wished them better luck next time and continued on without them.

So the country was split not by race, not by religion per se, not by economic class and not by region. There was a fundamental chasm between those who were determined to live in pursuit of their perception of an idyllic past, and those who knew the way to a better world was through social evolution.

Eliza worried.

She worried about Jane and the other teenagers Jane spent her time with. Not because they were self-indulging or selfish, but because they were so filled with the passion of youth and the great and certain conviction that there was no compromise between right and wrong, black and white.

They were convinced that any change to society lay squarely with them, and they were right. The young adults always carry the baggage of the past while holding the key to the future. Always and forever.

They wanted to run out and effect that change in a dramatic and explosive manner and they were wrong. Drama and explosions burn fast and then dissolve into cinders- it takes synchronized careful deliberate steps to effect lasting change.

She worried about her mother because she always looked so tired and frail, even though she knew her father always made sure she was safe and taking good care of herself.

Eliza loved the romantic yet tragic story that was her parents' history, but could only ask her father to repeat it- her mother never talked about it.

"Tell me, dad- tell me again…please".

And Gabriel would stop whatever he was doing and sit down next to Eliza, taking a moment to collect his thoughts before speaking.

"Well, I've known your mother a very long time- in fact, we were both your age when we met…" and he'd go on even though each telling brought up painful memories for him.

He'd felt it was important that his daughters knew about their mother, and that it would have the most impact if they first heard about it when they were the same age as Crispin had been when he'd met her…

…when he'd heard sobbing and the crashing of branches in the dark- heard it even though the windows to their house were closed against the chill of November.

Alarmed, but not afraid, he'd taken his dog and slipped out into the darkness; the forest closing silently behind them. It only took a few moments to find her, but it seemed much longer- her fear floating like clouds in the wind and pulling him, urging him forward.

She'd stopped running and his dog sped ahead of him nose in the air and white tail tip flagging, but he easily followed the sound of her muffled crying- a lost soul frantically trying to tuck her sanity back into herself before it disappeared forever.

Gabriel knew these woods backwards and forwards, daylight or midnight, but they were still treacherous with the thorny vines that covered everything and they caught his arms as he ran, but he didn't even feel it- he was compelled to help whoever was weeping in the black cavern of night.

So he ran surefooted between the trees and ignored when the thorns clawed at and ripped away the skin from his arms and hands and he skidded instinctively to a halt at the edge of the drop off- a sudden gulch over 50 ft deep that seemed to open up out of nowhere.

The girl, running scared and in the dark from the other direction, had not been so lucky.

Carefully, Gabriel shimmied down the steep embankment to where she lay being comforted by his floppy-eared beagle, her panic subsiding as it was drawn into and neutralized by the calm liquid brown eyes of the little tri-colored hound.

The girl looked up at him through tears. "I can't move my arm or leg. I can never go home. They killed my mother".

All three sentences were expressed matter of factly and without hysterics and he knew they were all rock solid truth.

Her arm was, in fact broken as well as her ankle.

She was covered in blood from the same thorns that had shed his own.

Her hands.

Her hands and arms were…charred? And her feet were bare save for a few tatters of slippers that seemed to be melted to them. Her feet and lower legs were as scorched as her hands and arms, and the tips of her hair smelled burnt. It'd been heated almost to combustion.

Gabriel had half carried, half supported her all the way back to their house, where his parents took her in and gently cleaned her up, gave her something to eat and made up a bed for her in their spare room. They asked nothing and offered comfort and safety.

By daybreak they knew what had happened.

News travels quickly in a rural area. Bad news even faster than that.

Crispin had no family other than her mother and Gabriel's parents petitioned the local authorities for her to stay with them. Having no other options and no one else fighting for the responsibility, it was granted without opposition or fanfare.

The townspeople were actually secretly relieved. If Crispin had stayed in their own community she'd be a constant reminder of what had happened.

Gabriel's family was from the next town over.

Their little town's population was 95% white.

The next town's was 95% black, like Gabriel's family.

One little homeless orphaned white girl would completely disappear and never have to be thought about or seen again even though the communities were less than 10 miles apart. There's a lot of woods and a cultural ocean between the two…no matter how advanced or enlightened the society claims it is.

So they had met, and they grew up together, and were inseparable. There was never a question in either one's heart that they would remain together always. And so they were.

Eliza always sighed at the end of the story- no pretend fairy tale could touch it for the perfection of it. Nothing in a book could have the impact of seeing how her parents still looked at each other. The absolute power of love was in front of her and her sister every day and the truth of the story etched in the scars both her parents wore- would always wear.

If Crispin's mother had been a free thinker and passionate advocate for those in positions of oppression- and she had been both- Crispin was a hundred times more.

The only way to avenge her mother's death was to never give up, never lose hope, and never stop fighting for those who could not.

Growing up in Gabriel's world and being constantly reminded that in America all men were created equal, but some were more equal than others only served to strengthen her resolve and cement her devotion to justice.

Crispin's goal in life was to save the world.

Gabriel's was to save Crispin.

And heaven help him- Crispin's daughters were exactly like her.

Jane had all the fire and none of the fear of having been burnt- mentally or otherwise. She was first in line at protests, first to run into danger to help someone being oppressed by a taunting mob, always first- leading with her heart before her head could catch up.

Eliza was the quiet one- no less intense, but just that much more cautious, intuitive, sensitive. She had early signs of being a healer and Gabriel stood guard over her talent until she was old enough to handle the pain being a healer would inflict on her.

Just as he stood guard over Jane and did his best to temper her temper with reason and patience, two things she had little use for, little time for.

Just as he stood guard over Crispin, always.

Eliza felt her mother's pain and could do nothing to help her.

Eliza felt…something in Jane and had no way of verbalizing what she sensed to anyone else. It didn't matter. The cancer growing in Jane would take her quickly and no matter what medical science could combat it with, even if they could have afforded medical care.

It was cold comfort and one more dragon for her mother to slay, for herself to battle, for Gabriel to shield against in vain.

The day Jane died, their friends and neighbors helped lay her to rest wrapped in an old quilt and lowered into the ground on a little knoll at the edge of a winding creek outside of town. Jane had come to this spot regularly; sitting under one particular tree, gathering both strength and her thoughts.

She laughed quietly and a little self-consciously when people teased her about 'her tree', but those who knew her best believed her when she said, "I feel her moving, I hear her breathing, I see her leaves and can smell her roots. It's not the biggest tree, not the strongest tree, not even the prettiest tree, but it's *my* tree".

So they laid her carefully between those roots and then gently tucked little tokens along with her- a few books that she'd loved, flowers, handwritten notes, everyone offering something for her travels to the next plane of existence.

One of her friends had been crying softly into Jane's "Superhero cape"- a shawl she'd found at a junk store and wore to every demonstration and action she went to. It fluttered down into the grave featherlike, then seemed to rise of its own accord and everyone gasped.

Kneeling at the side of her sister's last resting place, Eliza had plucked the shawl out of the air as it fell and it now rested lightly across her shoulders.

Quiet and shy by nature, Eliza's love for her sister demanded that she carry on in her stead. And so she would.

The Sanctuary was outwardly a community center, soup kitchen, halfway house and homeless shelter all rolled into one.

So it was perfectly normal to see all sorts of people coming and going at odd hours, some staying only a short while or a day and some seeming to move in more permanently. They were nothing to be alarmed about- just the dregs and scraps of an eroding society-old people, women and their children, cripples, ex-soldiers the military machine had chewed up and spit out damaged beyond repair, minorities of all stripes…just the wretched refuse of mankind.

Gabriel acted as the Sanctuary's coordinator, organized the donations and ran the kitchen- it was all donations that kept it going, but not like similar places used to be run. Those days of charity were over. People were expected to succeed or fail, live or die according to their own willpower. Handouts were for the weak, and the weak served no purpose but to drag down the strong.

 These donations came from the residents and passers by themselves- everyone who entered the doors brought something with them to share- tangible items like clothing and food as well as their own stories and experiences, skills and gifts.

The Sanctuary provided for the physical body as well as the human spirit- there is strength in numbers, power in community. Needs were met by each other, for each other.

On the face of it, it was the epitome of the success of the new government's tenets- bold libertarianism- god loved those who helped themselves.

What was really happening was socialism with a steel backbone and a determination to do what the rest of the world had said as it pulled the door quietly but firmly shut behind the US- "Better luck next time".

Luck had nothing to do with it, and everyone in the Sanctuary knew it. "Next time" was now, and they were going to make it reality.

Their elections had turned into exercises in futility; their power as individuals was gone. Even as a group, even if they could muster a HUGE group, they were no match for those in power. They still had options, however.

They could run away- what the former residents of the Sanctuary had done, and what those who couldn't or wouldn't form true inclusive communities had done- carve out little enclaves of 'like-minded individualists'. What did that even mean? It didn't even make sense. Those in power watched them go and laughed, knowing they'd spend all their time and energy imploding and disintegrating from within- they were no threat to anyone but themselves.

They voted anyway, of course. Eliza's parents took her to the polls and told her how very important it was for everyone to vote- how people before them had protested and petitioned, were beaten and jailed just for the right to vote and it disrespected all those who came before to shun it now. Because it would mean something again someday, as long as they all kept fighting.

Of course that was metaphorical. Anyone who thought they could take up arms against the gigantic standing army and police forces at the government's disposal was a fool, no matter how much hardware and ammo they had squirreled away over the years.

Every so often one of the reclusive militia groups would pour down from the mountains or erupt out of the woods and fling itself at the government in a heroic spectacle of sincerity before being decimated and forgotten about.

Every so often one of the religious encampments would send out human sacrifices carrying holy bibles who would scream at the government and point fingers and threaten god's wrath until they were carried away in straitjackets, never to be seen again.

No, fighting for change meant methodical, tiny, almost imperceptible cuts to the fabric of power.

That's what the Sanctuary was really about.

Eliza watched her father carry on the day to day running of the facility, while her mother met with the people coming and going- people who had news of what was going on in the rest of the country- news they couldn't get from the television or radio.

The media were owned and run by the government, no matter what various names they said were in charge. That was nothing new, it had been that way for years and cleverly set up so it looked like there were opposing viewpoints, when all it meant to do was keep Americans fighting among themselves and ignorant of what was really going on both at home and in the rest of the world. It was a brilliant success.

Proof of that was the stunned disbelief of the American public when they were cut off from the rest of the world. How could that happen? What had they done to merit such shoddy treatment?

Oh, sure- the USA was a great believer in sanctions- for other countries as 'we' saw fit. But for the rest of the world to institute sanctions on *us*? How dare they!

Had they forgotten how great we were? How we'd "saved their asses" in every war (never mind that we started most of them)? We were the Leader of the World!

The endless attacks on other nations, the nauseatingly limitless patriotic posturing and woefully misguided sense of superiority were so ingrained in the American psyche that they could no more recognize it for what it was than they could've swum to Mars.

The government told them, "Don't worry! We don't need those losers! We're *America* and we need no one!" as the country crumbled and faltered even further down the road to unimportance.

Those who listened to the government, the government media and the isolationists in the church and the militias were indoctrinated to always distrust their fellow Americans. So it lay at the feet of everyone else to finagle their country back where it was supposed to be- in the hands Of the People, By the People and For the People. *All* the People.

Crispin was a facilitator. She could sit in a room with several different personalities who each had different strengths, experiences and passions and pull them all together for a common action. Nothing big.

Big actions got noticed. Small actions were effective because they didn't even try to uproot an entire tree of power...just nip a tiny bud here and there.

Over half of the people coming to see Crispin were women with children. Older children always wanted to be part of whatever plans were being made.

Eliza would take the younger children over to one side of the room where they could still see their mothers and she'd keep them occupied with stories, puzzles, games, snacks or just sit and listen to them talk to her and each other about their own lives, fears and worries.

Many of the meetings and actions took place at night, and Eliza laid out bedding and stuffed toys and stayed with the children till their mothers came back for them. Her calm demeanor belied her young age and her little charges stayed with her willingly and happily.

Crispin herself didn't go out anymore- Gabriel had had to resort almost to tears, but finally she capitulated and stayed where he could keep an eye on her. Her friends and daughters also stressed that she was doing invaluable work that really couldn't be done by anyone else and so she stayed.

Eliza watched her mother's eyes follow those going out the door and into the world to make a difference with a mixture of longing and resignation- Gabriel was right, her strength was in remaining here.

Jane was not so easily dissuaded. Every day, every night, every minute until she was too sick to leave her bed Jane was at the front of every action. Marching and protesting, small acts of non-violent trespass, graffiti and vandalism- if it somehow made business as usual inconvenient or cumbersome for the government-protected and individual-screwing corporations, Jane was all over it.

She was tireless and fearless, and behaved as though every moment of her life needed to count for something, as if she knew somehow that her moments were numbered even more stingily than most people.

Eliza watched them both, and her father as well, with worry and love. All she had ever known- worry and love.

Today was different.

Today they were all in the kitchen together, preparing the holiday meal for everyone at the Sanctuary. No actions, no protests, no outside influences today. Today was all about community and being thankful.

The food, of course, had all been donated, and there was plenty to be sure, but not in a very 'traditional Thanksgiving' sort of way. After some thought and assessment of possibilities, Gabriel had announced, "And there shall be SOUP!" and began a furious chopping and mincing of ingredients.

Crispin made mounds of biscuits and Jane baked pan after pan of brownies. Eliza was setting the long tables when she stopped in mid-stride and started laughing.

Her entire family was flabbergasted- it was not a common thing for serious Eliza to find anything funny.

"SOUP!" Eliza crowed. "We're having SOUP for Thanksgiving!"

Gabriel started to chuckle along with Crispin and Jane shot out of the kitchen, returning a few minutes later with three smooth oval stones, which she carefully scrubbed, then wrapped up in netting and tied with a bow made of twine.

With much flourish, Jane lowered it into the soup just in time for everyone to arrive for dinner, and the reading of the story.

As the afternoon sunlight streamed through the stained glass windows, turning even the most humble dust mote into a microscopic rainbow, their little community sat at the post-dinner tables companionably and quietly, safely and securely without worry for one evening.

"Once upon a time an old woman trudged down a road in a strange country. She was a very long way from home. Besides being tired, she was hungry. In fact, she had eaten nothing for two days.

"How I would like a good dinner tonight, and a bed to sleep in," she thought.

Suddenly, ahead of her she saw the lights of a village.

"Maybe I'll find a bite to eat there, and a loft to sleep in," she said to herself.

Now the peasants of that place feared strangers. When they heard that a strange old woman was coming down the road, they talked among themselves.

"Why is she alone? Maybe she's a witch! Maybe not- maybe she's just an old woman alone. But we have little enough for ourselves." And they hurried to hide their food.

They pushed the sacks of barley under the hay in the lofts. They lowered buckets of milk down the wells.

They spread old quilts over the carrot bins. They hid their cabbages and potatoes under the beds. They hung their meat in the cellars.

They hid all they had to eat. Then – they waited.

The old woman stopped first at the house of Paul and Francoise.

"Good evening to you," she said. "Could you spare a bit of food for a hungry old woman?"

"We have had no food for ourselves for three days," said Paul. Francoise made a sad face. "It has been a poor harvest."

The old woman went on the house of Albert and Louise.

"Could you spare a bit of food? And have you some corner where I could sleep for the night?"

"Oh no," said Albert. "We gave all we could spare to people who came before you."

"Our beds are full," said Louise.

At Vincent and Marie's the answer was the same. It had been a poor harvest and all the grain must be kept for seed.

So it went all through the village. Not a peasant had any food to give away. They all had good reasons. One family had used the grain for feed. Another had an old sick father to care for. All had too many mouths to fill.

Sheri Dixon

The villagers stood in the street and sighed. The looked as hungry as they could.

The old woman thought a moment.

Then she called out, "Good people!" The peasants drew near.

"I am a hungry old woman in a strange land. I have asked you for food and you have no food. Well then, I'll have to make stone soup."

The peasants stared."

Eliza smiled to herself as the toddlers tucked in around her gasped at this part of the story, because they had just EATEN this self-same soup. They looked at her quizzically, skeptically, wanting to believe in miracles but afraid to all the same. She felt honored and a little overwhelmed that they looked up to her, looked straight to her for verification of things real and not real, dangerous and safe.

She had no illusions of power or immortality. She was a very tiny person as was everyone there in the Sanctuary.

Therein lay their strength- individually and outwardly they were no threat to anyone, especially those with money and power.

Far from causing them to despair and give up, they knew that meant that the path to reclaiming their country was wide open.

Reclamation- Crispin 2015

The secret to avoiding trouble was to avoid attracting attention.

The nation was under the thumb of the most vocal and inflexible among them, having first ignored them, then tolerated them, then suddenly (or so it seemed) being overrun by them.

But it wasn't sudden at all. It had taken several generations for this very abnormal and unhealthy state of affairs to become something people took for granted as just the way life was.

It all seemed so benign at the time. People had a right to different opinions- even if those opinions seemed pretty anti-social and mildly disturbing, this was still America and that's what we're all about here- accepting the odd duck and respecting the weird uncle.

Yes, everyone agreed that the 1st Amendment stated that we were to have no state religion, but what would it hurt to humor the Christians and allow things like nativity scenes on the courthouse lawn, slipping the mention of "god" into the Pledge and onto our money? If it made them happy, it was really no skin off of everyone else's nose, was it? Tolerance, and all that.

But what happened when they removed "E Pluribus Unum" from the money and inserted "In God We Trust"? There was a slight shift in attitude- imperceptible it seemed, but from that point on we were NOT reminded that "out of many, we've become One", but were told that there was only one god- at least only one that mattered enough to be put on our money.

Yes, the 2nd Amendment began with the words "well-regulated militia", not "every man for himself" but most of those good ol' boys seemed to know what they were doing and were just having fun with their toys. Besides, they looked so pitiful when they pouted.

But somehow the 2nd Amendment was tweaked and twisted and went from being something that guaranteed that each state have its own well-regulated and trained militia to fight *for* the government if needed, to having literally millions of people heavily armed with no training, no organization and precious few restrictions who had the idea that their job, nay; their destiny, was to be prepared to fight *against* the government.

When and how and why that was going to happen, they weren't sure. But they would be ready.

The more deeply imbedded in the fabric of society the vengeful God and the gun culture became, instead of being purer and safer, the more sinful and dangerous society became.

Oh, it wasn't only the fault of those two. Simultaneously, the very wealthy and powerful were climbing ever higher up the financial ladder and hauling it up behind them.

These weren't the doctors or lawyers or other workaday wealthy. They weren't on the covers of the entertainment magazines and their names were not household words. Indeed, they were so far removed from society what they were doing wasn't even considered by them as anything untoward. It was just good business sense.

It was good business sense to force plants and animals to produce quickly and abundantly. What could it matter if it was unnatural and needed chemical support to keep them alive till harvested?

It was good business sense to purchase politicians and judges who could then draft up laws that favored them. Very expedient, exceedingly smooth.

It was good business sense to scnd jobs overseas- lower wages and no pesky safety or environmental regulations, and then to stash profits in off-shore accounts.

It was good business sense to strip the planet of resources- slash and burn and never look back. The earth is pretty big; it'll take care of itself.

It was good business to finance new pharmaceuticals, and then sell to a society sick from genetically modified foods, unemployed or having to work multiple low paying jobs just to survive, toxic from the fractured environment.

And very good business to sell them insurance- collect the premiums and then deny them care for any number of official sounding yet totally bogus reasons.

This wasn't some close-knit group planning a cohesive social takeover- the phantom straw man of the "New World Order" was just another diversion, a shell game for the huddled masses clutching their bibles and their guns.

These people were not inherently bad. They did not wake up every morning and think excitedly, "Who am I going to ruin today?" but because they were so far removed from…anyone else, it just didn't matter.

Those other people were not underfoot, they did not appear in their dining room looking unemployed, hungry, scared. They weren't looking in their windows, homeless, hopeless, dying.

They were numbers, statistics, and liabilities.

Of course they knew they were 'out there'. That's why they'd been marketing to them. For several generations, now.

The marketing was subtle and overwhelmingly unobtrusive.

Like all marketing it was designed to sell things.

More importantly, it was designed to sell ideas.

And since they had very deep pockets, they could afford the very best marketers.

So Americans came to believe that no where no how no way was any place better than America. That America had come up with every great idea, ever, and didn't need to look outside our borders for anything new. That if you even whispered that something may be better somewhere else, well then, you just needed to up and move there, you ungrateful bastard.

Meanwhile, American foods were not welcome overseas because they were unsafe, and people overseas lived longer, worked fewer hours and were much more rested and happy than Americans.

The people who had ignored the 1st Amendment were encouraged to be bolder, more vocal and more intolerant of anyone not following their religion's rules. There were pickets and demonstrations by the most extreme factions against almost absolutely anyone else, but instead of reining them in and reminding them about the 1st Amendment, the others who claimed the same faith looked the other way. At most they said, "Well, we don't agree with them".

But they let it go on.

The people who had twisted the 2nd Amendment became sort of fanatical and a little creepy, hoarding weapons and ammo furtively yet loudly and belligerently screaming *"No Compromise!"* whenever anyone dared to mention any sort of regulations or safeguards or questioned their warped interpretation of the amendment.

They were goaded into even more suspicious hysteria by a constant and accelerating deluge of propaganda and hype the type of which had not been seen in many years. There was so much danger from so many sources that they could *never* own enough weaponry to stave it off...but they tried.

Oh, they tried.

They stockpiled and packed their homes full of an arsenal fit for a king...or a terrorist cell. All loaded, of course, and within easy reach. Because *Second Amendment!*

And the hunters and sports shooters and other non-rabid gun owners shook their heads and said, "I guess they're a few beers short of a six pack, but they're actually pretty good guys."

And they let it go on.

Politicians stood up and announced that they consulted God and the Holy Bible before the

Constitution when making decisions, and no one told them they were wrong; on the contrary, many people used only that criterion to judge who to vote for.

Several state constitutions specified that to hold office you *must* believe in the Christian God, and no one stood up to insist that that was wrong and very *un*-American.

There was a push to teach schoolchildren that a story in a book of faith was just as scientific as…science. And in many places it passed as law without anyone telling them that that was wrong- faith belongs in church and science belongs in school.

And so it began. And it grew and grew and the folks who weren't right in the Heart of It and could see it happening had no idea.

Those in the South and in the rural pockets of everywhere else could see it- for those who were in favor of All God All Guns All the Time and Everywhere it was a very good place to be and they fed on each other's fanaticism and fear and hatred and gained strength and momentum and numbers.

Those who were not in favor became alarmed and voted against all of it and were shunned and mocked and spat on. They tried to warn the rest of the country- tell them the dangers that were coming, but no one believed them.

They watched as over and over again laws were being overturned that granted freedom to people and laws enacted that limited or eliminated freedom.

It was believed sincerely that hard-won freedoms of the past- for women and minorities and gays and all other groups not white and Christian had been a horrible mistake that god was now punishing us for and the politicians and church leaders pushed and pushed to take all that back- take America back- all the way back to the early 1900's when "traditional America" was a great place to be…if you were white and Christian and male and straight.

The rest of the country insisted that it was only a few "vocal lunatic fringe" types and naught to worry about.

By cover of night, the ranks of the Ku Klux Klan and other white supremacist groups swelled again and spread from the South to the North- a dark and rancid oil spill of hatred fanned by the frustrations of the economy and the empty promises of their leaders that "Everything was great back before we gave all these people too much freedom" and they made life a living hell for non-whites, and women, and gays.

Minorities of all varieties began to move away from the worst areas, and an underground railroad of sorts rose from the ranks of those who still knew right from wrong and what it meant to be an American who believed in equality for everyone, or a Christian who followed the teachings of Christ- rose to meet them and help them on their way to safety.

At first Crispin's mother was very vocal about the way things were going in their pocket of the south, and not in a complimentary way.

The locals would've stopped eating in her restaurant, but the food was too good.

Southerners are nothing if not big fans of dinner.

Everyone waited for cooler heads to step up and slap down the 'lunatic fringe' but they didn't. One ridiculous ruling and law after the other and suddenly it was too late- the fringe had become the mainstream.

And then things really advanced.

The Congress and Senate and White House were in the course of just a few election cycles all extreme Right conservatives, thanks to clever marketing to the frightened and over-worked base and creative gerrymandering of the voting districts.

The corporations and churches packed DC with lobbyists and one by one every single Amendment fell except the 2nd, which was re-written to read

"A Godly and well-armed populace being necessary to guard against tyranny, the right of all individuals to own, carry and trade any form of arms shall not be infringed."

The gun owners watched suspiciously for any tyrannical activity but ignored anything at all that didn't directly threaten their personal arsenals.

The corporate takeover of their government? Not a peep.

The discrimination of the women and minorities? Not a flicker of interest.

The destruction of the entire rest of the Constitution and Bill of Rights? Sound of crickets.

The country was under the thumb of God and Guns.

The flag still waved and they still mouthed the words of the Pledge, but inside most people knew.

America was gone.

As things progressed, the only prudent thing was to go silent. Try to do what they could in the face of ever-growing insanity, but as far under the radar as possible.

Crispin and her mother lived out in the woods a few miles from a small town.

A very small house- not much more than what hunters used on their leased properties- on a very small piece of ground, there were a few acres of forest and about an acre of clearing in the middle where the house and garden and small barn sat.

They grew most of their own food because they liked doing it and they didn't need much- some vegetables and fruits, eggs from a flock of about half a dozen hens, milk from 3 long-eared Nubian goats, and meat from the extra roosters who always managed to hatch out with the new hens from the nests that were brooded several times a year.

Crispin was home schooled, but not for the reason most of those around them did it.

While most home schooled children were kept at home to shelter them from the dangers of the outside world- outside of the church building, anyway- Crispin's mother believed that a school room couldn't possibly provide *enough* variety for a child to absorb and experience.

And, having no one else in the world- they just liked each other's company and saw no good reason for the separation of an artificially-designated school year.

Far from being hermits. Crispin and her mother traveled often- long road trips stopping off at the homes of friends and acquaintances, people from every walk of life and in every type of setting from large cities to huge isolated ranches and everything in between.

So many ideas, ways of living, culture and foods- the world was a wonderful place and Crispin and her mother embraced it all.

In their little town or on the road, Crispin never heard anyone call her mother anything but "Mama".

When she lost her job due to 'downsizing', which was really just code for "We can hire 2 new people for less than what we pay you because you know what you're doing", Mama took what little nest egg they had and rented out a tiny store front in town- one of those places that seems to be a different thing every month, a cursed little building where no business thrived. The last tenant had set it up as a restaurant.

Mama went in with an idea and a plan and set about making it work.

Before long, "Mama's Kitchen" opened up. The sign boasted, "Authentic Home-style Cuisine".

There was a notice at the door directing, "Close the door behind you- no slamming it shut, and take your shoes off, I just mopped".

Several wooden picnic tables provided diners with a place to eat, after surveying the daily offering- there was no menu.

On a chalkboard over the counter that separated the kitchen from the dining room was the vittles du jour. Mama's Kitchen opened up about 11 and shut down by 6, and there was only one thing on the board every day. Sometimes spaghetti and meatballs, sometimes pot roast and gravy, sometimes cornbread and black-eyed peas, and sometimes even breakfast for dinner…whatever Mama decided to cook was what diners were expected to eat.

There was a table off to the side with the fixin's for peanut butter and jelly sandwiches for anyone who didn't like what Mama had to offer.

Small placards on each table stated, "Come on up and help yourself- be sure to go wash up first, and remember to take your dishes back to the sink- I'm really not your mama".

The food was set out buffet-style, with a big sign over the vegetables stating that consumption of veggies was prerequisite to getting dessert.

From day one it was a very popular place. So popular that Mama and Crispin could take off every few months for a week or so and do their traveling. Their neighbors cared for their livestock and their customers learned to accept good-naturedly the, "Gone for a spell- go home and feed yourself" shade pulled down over the window of the front door.

As successful as "Mama's Kitchen" was, and as friendly as everyone was to both Mama and Crispin there was always just a little distance between them because after all, Mama wasn't from around 'here'. Mama had moved to the small town from somewhere up north, and that was a tough row to hoe in the South.

The saying went "If you are from the North, and come to visit, you're a Yankee. If you come to *stay*, you're a Damn Yankee". In a culture that based its opinion of you on the first two questions anyone got asked-
"Who's your mama's people?" and "Where's your church home?" it was difficult to fit in when you had no acceptable answer for either one.

No one knew 'their people' of course- they were Damn Yankees.

And they didn't attend church. Ever.

Mama had been there for going on 20 years now, but would always be just a bit of an outsider. Crispin had been born in the little town, fatherless but well-loved, confident and self-assured.

"Crispin? How you doin', baby?"

"Just fine, Miz McLeroy- how are you today?"

Crispin brought out the older woman's drink without being asked to- sweet tea, extra ice, and one lemon wedge. Just like every other day. Miz McLeroy was well into her 80's but sharp as a tack. Folks said that Mr. McLeroy just up and decided to die one day from the weariness of being poked by that sharpness for over half a century. The coroner had said heart attack, but you never could tell.

The old woman inspected her tea carefully, found it to her liking and turned her attention to Crispin. "Honey, you look so lonely in here with just your mama keeping you company- wouldn't you like to go to school with the other children? My granddaughters would love to be friends with you…at school".

"No, ma'am- I'm fine right here but thank you. I've seen your granddaughters and they're beautiful. Someday I hope to be just like them".

Crispin turned to hide her grimace and looked straight up into the face of Miz Ponder, who came to eat with Miz McLeroy every single day. Miz Ponder winked and grinned and sat down across from Miz McLeroy. "Lordy, Ida- why do you wart the poor child so? It's easy to see that she's doing just fine the way she is".

Setting the cup of hot black coffee down in front of Miz Ponder, Crispin mouthed "Thank you" to her and smiled before going to fetch the women's dinners for them.

Watching the young girl heaping mcat loaf, mashed potatoes, gravy, and a sweet corn/pepper medley onto their plates, Coralee Ponder said to no one and everyone in particular, "She's a lovely little thing, isn't she? So polite and smart- just like her mama".

Ida's lips pursed but she managed a weak smile. "It's a shame that they're not Christians- we could use both of their lovely voices in the choir".

"It's none of our business *what* they are", Coralee chided, "What matters is that they're good people, and they are good people through and through".

"That's not what the Good Book says, and it's not what Brother Amos says…" and then Ida was abruptly cut off by her friend.

"Good lord, Ida- the Good Book says nothing of the sort and Brother Amos hasn't been here long enough to know his chin from a hole in the ground when it comes to our community and who is in it! Now you're going to spoil my lunch, and then I'll be really cross with you, so hush!"

Coralee smiled sincerely at Crispin headed their way even as uttering the last words to Ida. She and Ida had been best friends for 70+ years. Ida was a good woman, but lands, she got stubborn about the strangest things. It was best to just let it go.

Ever since Ida's husband passed, she spent more and more time depending on the companionship of others. Coralee had a huge assortment of children, grandchildren and great-grandchildren, and her home and life were filled with them all routinely, but Ida was an only child and had a strained at best relationship with her own children and grandchildren. When she became a widow, she was truly alone.

She had lunch with Coralee every day and that helped.

Every morning she did her 'church time'- a faithful member of the Altar Guild, Ida went to the church every day to polish the candlesticks, dust the altar, vacuum the carpeting around the pulpit, wash the window glass on the doors…whatever needed done in her opinion to keep the Lord's House in order. She'd been told that it was only really necessary Monday and Thursday mornings- the mornings after the church services- but she didn't mind going every day.

She talked to the Lord while she worked, and if he was there, she talked to the preacher.

Brother Amos had come from Alabama just recently. He replaced Brother Travis, who'd decided to step down on his 80th birthday and relocate to Pensacola to minister to the other residents of the Royal Palms RV Park in between cribbage tournaments and bocce ball.

While Brother Travis had grown up in their town and had known all the families and their members, all the quirks and idiosyncrasies inherent in any population, Brother Amos came filled with the fire of Absolute Righteousness burning in his eyes.

Even though the congregation was 100% conservative fundamentalist Bible literalists, Brother Travis kept them all on an even keel- encouraging them to show grace and compassion to their brothers and sisters, not only in their own flock, but the rest of the world in general. "Love the sinner, hate the sin" was his motto, along with "Only God can judge".

And so they did for years and years- the little white church was host to dinners and fundraisers for all members of the community, not just their own circle of families. Their goal was to bring souls to Jesus through word AND deed- spreading the Good News to all with love, not aggression; inclusion, not exclusion.

Now there were murmurs and rumblings from within with every Sunday sermon admonishing them to "Seek out and cut from thyself anyone who is an abomination to the Lord our God- for lo the body may bleed and the heart may hurt from it but the price is your Eternal Life or Eternal Damnation!"

Bit by bit, congregant by congregant the flock was purged and cleansed in an effort to glow like the candlesticks Ida polished till her fingers ached.

TammyJo Wilson? The daughter of Tammy and Joe Wilson? Fifteen and 'in trouble'.

Be gone.

And she was sent to the home for unwed mothers to await the arrival of her precious package from God, which she would then deliver to presumably loving adoptive parents.

Clarence and Roy, both in their 50's and 4th generation local boys were upstanding, and employed, and homeowners, and Christians, and gay as the day was long.

Be gone.

And they were excommunicated and shunned.

The list went on and on- the ones who'd been divorced, the ones who were 'living in sin', and the ones who drank alcohol or encouraged their children to believe in evolution.

Be gone.

And that was just inside the church doors- outside contained a bottomless pit of sinners who needed to be guarded against.

Amos learned early on that a prime source of information concerning the entire congregation and beyond was Ida. She talked. He listened.

Amos also learned early on that the place to eat in town was Mama's Kitchen.

"Have a seat wherever you like, sir- the fixin's for today are listed up on the board, help yourself when you're ready. What can I fetch you to drink?" the little girl smiled when he walked in the door.

"Well, young lady, I'm new here. I'd be ever so honored if you'd set with me while I eat", Amos grinned a cherubic smile that would cause the angels to break out into song and elicit the trust of even the most jaded of characters. He'd practiced in front of a mirror for years and was right proud of that smile.

Crispin asked her mother if it would be okay for her to take a short break to make the new preacher feel at home and Mama said, "Of course, dear".

So she gathered up a small dish of spaghetti and meatballs, garlic bread and salad and sat across from Brother Amos, who'd piled his plate high and was busily working his way through it.

Between bites he asked, "Why aren't you in school?"

"Because my mama home schools me".

"Ah, a very good idea- the world is an evil place filled with evil things".

Crispin thought a moment before answering with a frown, "I'm sorry, but Mama and I don't find that to be true- we travel all over and far as I can tell, the world is a beautiful place filled with beautiful people".

"Where's your daddy?"

"I don't know- I've never met him".

"You and your ma live all alone?"

"Sometimes. Sometimes we have friends who stay with us on their way to somewhere else."

"Where do you go to church?"

"We don't go to church. Mama says the Earth is our Mother and we are all brothers and sisters".

Brother Amos made much of finishing his dinner, patted Crispin on the head, tipped her generously, waved to her mother and left.

The next day he started asking Ida about them.

Amid many little, "Tsk, tsk" noises Ida told Brother Amos about Crispin and her mother- how they weren't 'really' from around there, and how they seemed to be nice enough (and Lord knew the mother could cook), but it was such a shame that poor little Crispin didn't know Jesus, that all she had was that mother with traveling gypsy blood, and that ever-changing herd of outcasts out at their place instead of a real Christian family and upbringing.

Brother Amos' head tipped just a bit to one side. "Outcasts? What outcasts?"

Ida sighed and whispered conspiratorially, even though they were alone in the church.

She mentioned the two other little houses on the farm, and that they were usually occupied by…travelers-black folks and Mexicans, which wouldn't have been so terribly bad, but also Muslims and *Gays*. All people headed away from the ruralness of the area and to larger centers of populations where there was more tolerance for their types. The really uppity ones who had money and/or knew someone overseas flat up and left the country. "And good riddance," Ida finished with a sniff.

Brother Amos had gained popularity and grace in the church through careful planning, expert politics and a flair for the dramatic. He was known to shake things up in sleepy little parishes. A congregation who could see without doubt that the Will of God was being done in an Old Testament manner was a congregation that was eager to tithe generously.

The Bible says you reap what you sow. Also known as you get what you pay for.

The church in Alabama where he'd just come from had taken a stand against the public schools, who were still teaching evolution as theory in science class instead of creationism.

One day Brother Amos had marched on the school with a Bible in one hand and a gun in the other, followed by a large group of incensed parishioners. They demanded all the science books be brought outside to the yard in front of the flagpole.

The science books were piled up, doused with gasoline and set aflame while Brother Amos preached to the gathered crowd- his voice timber strong and carefully modulated to bring out the best Fire and Brimstone possible, sparks and flames as a backdrop.

It was spectacular.

Crispin and her mother finished up the dishes at the restaurant and made sure it was all clean for the next day. Even though it was a holiday, her mother had insisted they be open. "Some of our neighbors are by themselves, we can have our holiday dinner with them right here", her mother had smiled.

Turkey, stuffing, cranberry sauce, mashed potatoes and gravy, pies made of pumpkin, pecans and apples- all day they had been serving a non-stop parade of their fellow townspeople.

Back at home, they curled up in front of the fire with cups of cocoa and prepared to read their traditional Thanksgiving story.

The clock ticked quietly while the fire hissed warmly, casting enough light to read by.

Opening the book and tucking it between them, her mother read the opening sentence.

Outside, the dogs barked a warning…and didn't stop.

Crispin held the book while her mother went to see what was wrong.

Outside, the yard was filled with the headlights of cars and trucks. Crispin set the book down and went out onto the porch to stand beside her mother.

Her mother had locked the dogs up as a courtesy to her guests- it seemed the entire congregation of the little church was in her yard.

Several of the men unloaded wood from the beds of their trucks and laid them out as for a bonfire around a center pole. "How can I help you?" Crispin's mother asked calmly.

Brother Amos strode to the front of the small crowd, a Bible in one hand and a gun in the other.

"Sister! You have been chosen by the Lord God Almighty to witness to these fine people on this glorious Thanksgiving night! Tell us your devotion to the One God Above!"

Crispin looked up at her mother nervously but her mother gently squeezed her shoulder in reassurance and strength.

"Brother Amos- you know full well that while I respect your beliefs and those of all my friends here in my yard, I believe in Mother Earth and the Infinite Circle of Life."

"Brothers, please help this woman to the stake so she can see the obvious errors of her ways".

Crispin's mother smiled at her reassuringly and nodded for her to stay on the porch- she had seen and heard many a snake oil salesman in her day and this one was clearly ridiculous. There were at least thirty people all standing there- the faces of everyone she had served daily. She saw Coralee and Ida off to one side. Ida had a small smile on her face that was strained and nervous and Coralee looked positively vexed.

She was escorted to the stake, and her hands tied behind her loosely and gently.

It was all for show, of course.

"Sister- I ask you- do you or do you not harbor all types of people who are abominations in the Lord's eyes? Give them food and shelter and aid them on their way to God knows where?"

Looking directly into Brother Amos' eyes, her answer came clearly and strong, though her smile remained open and sincere. "Brother Amos- I harbor all Nature's children both in my home and at my restaurant. You yourself dine there regularly, and though I disagree with you on many topics, I'd hardly call you an abomination".

Brother Amos' face turned red and his eyes narrowed.

There were murmurs from the crowd, and stifled chuckles.

He'd have to step up his game if he wanted to remain in charge.

There was no way he would be upstaged by a heathen…and a woman.

Grabbing the can of gasoline he liberally doused the wood at her feet intoning, "In the name of the Father, the Son and the Holy Ghost- I command you to forsake your evil ways and give yourself to the Lord our God!"

The congregation became silent. The only sound was Crispin on the porch, who had begun to gasp with each breath. Her mother still smiled at her. And winked.

Her voice remained clear and calm with no anger or sarcasm. She was herself- gracious and kind.

"Amos? I think you've taken your dog and pony show about as far as it's going to go. I believe what I believe and you believe what you believe. All these folks have known me for almost 20 years and they've known my daughter her entire life. We're good people and everyone here knows it. I'm not going to lie to neatly tie up your little exercise in fanatical devotion. It's over. You've had your fun, but it's over."

Brother Amos could sense the eyes of all the people behind him waiting for his next move. He heard feet shuffling nervously, losing interest.

He felt his congregation slipping away from him.

Not God. Him.

He threw the Bible onto the ground in order to reach into his pocket for a lighter. He lit one end of a gas-soaked stick and he slowly held it up to her face. "Woman, the Lord God says you are to be meek and obedient. Obviously, you are neither".

"*AMOS!*" Coralee's voice was sharp and commanding. He whipped around to face the old woman. "Did you not hear me? Women are to be meek and obedient!" and he shoved her to the ground next to the Bible.

Without a sound Ida rushed up and pushed Amos from behind and they both tripped and fell forward.

The flaming stick jammed into the gasoline soaked wood and as if by struck by lightning all three were instantly engulfed.

Brother Amos clutched Sister Ida and they rolled clear of the flames. He needed to untie the woman at the stake quickly- he'd never intended to hurt her, or anyone.

People had rushed forward and were slapping at the flames still licking their clothing and he struggled to get forward, to untie Crispin's mother.

Crispin!

Through the flames he saw the child standing in the fire frantically trying to untie her mother, who was almost unconscious from the black smoke billowing around her and the conflagration surrounded them both in an eerily dark yet brilliant halo from hell.

He spun around and struggled violently to get clear of the congregants and there was a sudden *CRACK*!

He had forgotten the gun was still in his hand.

Crispin's mother slumped forward and was still.

Time stopped. Everyone in the yard was lit by firelight and frozen in horror for one awful instant.

Then everyone was screaming and Brother Amos was yelling, "My God, I'm sorry! I'm so very sorry! It was an accident! I never meant to hurt anyone!"

Crispin couldn't blink or move, couldn't take her eyes off of her mother's face, till she realized that she herself was on fire. She leapt out of the flames and rolled on the ground till all she could smell was dirt and burnt flesh. Her own and her mother's. The people were coming towards her silently and in slow motion with their kind yet terrible faces.

People she'd known her whole life.

People who had just killed her mother.

Ignoring the pain in her hands and arms, her feet and legs, she ran.

Away from the stench. Away from what was left of her mother and their home. Away.

The last words her mother had spoken to her before their life ended echoed over and over in her head as she ran-

"Once upon a time..."

"We owe our children – the most vulnerable citizens
in any society –
a life free from violence and fear."
— Nelson Mandela

"Violence is the last refuge of the incompetent."
— Isaac Asimov

"Another world is not only possible, she is on her
way.
On a quiet day I can hear her breathing"
--Arundhati Roy

Sheri Dixon lives with her family in a log cabin on a small family farm in East Texas.

Together they strive to live lightly on the land and educate others to do the same- nothing is as important as environment and community for they are literally our Home and Family.

"American Evolution- Adolescence of a Nation" is the author's defiant response to being told over and over again that she's naïve and simple regarding reality...by grownups who are reading about and preparing for the Zombie Apocalypse.

Nothing is written in stone. When the shit hits the fan, people *are* just as liable to act with courage and grace as with fear and violence.

It happens every day.

Please visit Sheri at www.sheri-dixon.com

www.ingramcontent.com/pod-product-compliance
Lightning Source LLC
Chambersburg PA
CBHW071322130626
46556CB00004B/1710